M000036412

One Summer Day

USA TODAY BESTSELLING AUTHOR

Heather B. Moore

One Summer Day

A Prosperity Ranch Novel

Copyright © 2020 by Heather B. Moore
Print edition
All rights reserved

No part of this book may be reproduced in any form whatsoever without
prior written permission of the publisher, except in the case of brief passages
embodied in critical reviews and articles. This is a work of fiction. The
characters, names, incidents, places, and dialogue are products of the
author's imagination and are not to be construed as real.

Interior design by Cora Johnson
Edited by JL Editing Services and Lisa Shepherd
Cover design by Rachael Anderson
Cover image credit: Deposit Photos #11171940
Published by Mirror Press, LLC

ISBN: 978-1-947152-79-3

One Summer Day

She's desperate to start over. He represents the past she wants to leave behind. But falling in love is never about logic.

Macie's divorce has left her at rock-bottom, and she uproots everything and takes her young daughter to visit Prosperity Ranch for the summer. Every kid deserves to know her grandparents, right? Macie hopes for some healing time, even if she is staying at her ex in-laws' ranch. What she isn't expecting is her ex-husband's brother, Holt Prosper, to fit every ideal she's ever hoped for in a man.

1

"TWO-THOUSAND IS ALL I'm asking."

Holt Prosper shook his head even though his brother Knox couldn't see him on the other end of the phone call. "That's what you said last month," Holt said. "If I lend you another two-thousand dollars, you'll be in deep four thousand."

"But they put me on Granger," Knox said. "You know that bull throws everyone. The rodeo judging was rigged in Montana."

Holt couldn't hold back his scoff. His brother always had one sorry excuse after another. He'd chased his dream of becoming a big rodeo star, but that dream hadn't gone so well. He had yet to qualify for the pro circuit. Somehow, Knox had weaseled his inheritance from their dad, blown through it, gotten the girl, even married her, and now they had a kid together.

And now, Holt was standing in the living room of his family home, keeping everything together, being the go-to person in the family as usual. "I don't know, Knox," he said. The late-night call from his brother should have been warning enough. "Mom and Dad would be furious if they found out, and I don't think I can keep four thousand under the radar."

Holt had stayed back in Texas—Prosperity Ranch to be exact—and managed the ranch for their dad. His younger siblings were off to college, following their own ambitions. Holt wasn't one to complain. He loved the ranch. But he hated being everybody's fall-back guy. Especially Knox's.

"I'm sending half of it to Macie," Knox said, "if that makes you feel better."

At the mention of Macie's name, Holt physically reacted. He should be over it by now. The gut-punch, the racing thoughts, the slow-burn of his pulse. Macie was . . . His gaze involuntarily strayed to the family picture taken at Knox and Macie's wedding. Four years ago.

Holt rubbed his forehead, which did nothing to dispel his growing headache. "Are you ever going to tell me why you divorced her? And don't tell me what you told Mom."

Knox laughed.

Sometimes Holt hated his brother. It was complicated. The Macie staring back at him right now was how he remembered her from their first meeting when she'd come to the town of Prosper that was named after his great-grandfather and attended the hometown rodeo. Holt had even talked to her first. She'd been sweet, curious. Beautiful. Full of questions and smiles. He'd been about to ask her to the dance that followed the rodeo when Knox's name was called as the next bull rider.

Holt had told Macie that Knox was his brother, and the old saying *the rest was history* turned out to be a real thing. It wasn't the first time Knox had attracted a girl Holt had been interested in. But it was the first time Holt had cared.

"First of all," Knox drawled in a tone he usually saved for the ladies, "*I* didn't divorce Macie. *She* divorced *me*."

Holt tore his gaze from Macie's photo, which was mocking him with her dark brown eyes and stunning smile. He pushed out a breath. "And why's that? I thought you were her dream cowboy."

Another laugh from Knox sent heat pricking the back of Holt's neck.

"Tell you what, bro," Knox said with amusement. "Why don't you ask her for yourself? She'll be there tomorrow."

Holt stilled. It felt as if someone was dragging hot needles along his skin. "What are you talking about?"

"Didn't Mom tell you?"

If there was one thing about Knox that drove Holt the *most* crazy it was his inability to answer a question directly. Right now, though, it was imperative that Holt get his shock under control. He couldn't let his brother know how his thoughts had strayed to Macie more than once, both during her marriage to Knox, and well, now.

"Mom's been preoccupied," Holt said. With cancer treatments. And now Macie's visit might put a strain on his mom's health. She always went all-out for guests at the ranch.

Knox's next words were contrite. "Yeah, I know. Mom said she'd pick up Macie and Ruby at the airport. But, you know, if she's not feeling well, I was thinking . . ."

Another pet peeve of Holt's about his brother. Knox never asked things directly. He was a super-human-passive-aggressive type. If there was such a thing. "I'll pick them up." His tone might have come out casual, nonchalant even, but inside, all kinds of thoughts and emotions were brewing.

On second thought, maybe his dad could do the airport run.

"Thanks, man," Knox replied. "About the two-thousand. I really need it by tomorrow, or Friday at the very latest."

Holt closed his eyes. Exhaled. He had his own savings

account that was separate from the ranch funds. He'd been slowly renovating a house in town. Every penny counted. "All right."

He could hear the grin in his brother's reply.

"Thanks, Holt," Knox said. "I'll make good on it, I swear."

Holt only grunted and hung up. His twisting gut told him there was little chance of Knox paying back the original two-thousand, let alone this new loan.

He slipped the phone into the back pocket of his well-worn jeans. Then he scrubbed a hand through his hair, which had been confined beneath a cowboy hat most of the day. "Macie," he said, testing the word out on his tongue.

The last time he'd seen his sister-in-law—now ex-sister-in-law—had been when she'd been pregnant with Ruby. It had been Christmas time, and Knox brought his wife home for the holidays. Macie had spent more time in the bathroom than anywhere else in the house.

Then on Christmas Eve, Knox and their dad had gotten into another argument—about money, it was always about money—and Knox had packed up his and Macie's things. And that was that.

"So . . . Macie," Holt murmured to the picture. "Looks like I'm going to be moving back to my place sooner than I thought."

No matter how much time had passed, or how much he or Macie had changed, Holt Prosper knew one thing. He'd have to return to his partially-finished house sooner than he thought. He couldn't be sleeping in the same house as her.

2

MACIE SCRUBBED OUT THE orange stain in the middle of her skirt that her daughter had left after squishing a handful of goldfish crackers, stuffing them into her mouth all at once, then wiping her hand on Macie's skirt. The flight from San Diego to San Antonio had been eventful to say the least.

"I need help, Mommy!" Ruby called, her little voice echoing in the airport bathroom.

"Okay, baby, I'm coming."

"I'm not a baby," Ruby pouted.

Macie sighed to herself, tossed the wet paper towel into the garbage, and went to the bathroom stall. "Can you open it, sweetie?"

The door rattled, then opened. Ruby looked up at her, her brown eyes wide, both her sandals off. She'd pulled the red ribbon from her curly brown hair, which was well on its way to becoming dark like Macie's.

"Remember, you don't have to take off your shoes when you use the potty." Macie hid a smile. Ruby was a sensitive kid, and literal about everything, so Macie always had to watch how she said things or Ruby would throw one of her famous fits.

Okay, so they were temper tantrums, and Ruby should have grown out of them by now. Three going on four was way too old to lay down in the middle of a post office and kick and scream because Macie hadn't let her put a stamp on an envelope.

"The potty's too big," Ruby said, looking dubiously at the porcelain bowl.

"You're a big girl, now," Macie said. "Plus, Mommy can hold you, okay?"

Ruby bit her lip. "Okay."

Once they were out of the bathroom, shoes back on, ribbon retied, stain mostly removed on Macie, she felt like she'd crossed some kind of finish line. Now to get to baggage claim, and then out to the curb where her ex-mother-in-law, Heidi Prosper, would be there to meet them.

It was strange to be heading to the town of Prosper again. The last time she'd been to her in-laws' ranch was when she was pregnant with Ruby. That had ended in a disaster, and her husband had refused to go back home. Amazing the new freedoms that divorce had granted her.

Meeting Knox all those years ago had been a whirlwind. She'd been nearly twenty, he twenty-two, and she'd been swept up by the novelty of the champion bull rider paying attention to her. When Knox had asked her to the dirt dance, Macie had barely gathered her wits about her and answered yes.

She'd said goodbye to the first cowboy she'd met, Holt, then went along with Knox to the dance. Which consisted of . . . yep, dancing in the dirt. Macie was a city girl herself, but the small town of Prosper had been charming.

Everyone knew Knox, and as he held her in his arms, swaying to soulful country music, it seemed that half the town stopped by to congratulate him. Finally, Knox had looked at her with those brilliant green eyes of his and said, "Let's get out of here, sugar. Too many people. What do ya say?"

"Mommy." Ruby's voice broke apart Macie's memories. Her daughter tugged on her hand. "I wanna lollipop."

Macie blinked and looked to where Ruby was pointing to a young boy with one of those giant lollipops from an amusement park. "I don't think they sell those at the airport," she said, digging into her handbag, hoping she still had at least a fruit snack left. But there was nothing. The flight from San Diego had been exhausting since Ruby had missed her nap and wouldn't fall asleep on the plane.

"Maybe we can stop at the store with Grandma and get you a treat if you're a good girl," Macie said.

Ruby wasn't listening. She tugged away from Macie, who had to tighten her grasp on her hand.

"Look, Ruby!" Macie said, desperate to distract her daughter. "It's our suitcases. Can you help me get them?"

The diversion was only temporary, though, because after Macie lugged the two suitcases and the tagged booster seat off the conveyer belt, Ruby was in tears.

"It's no f-f-fair," she cried. "I was a good girl on the p-p-plane."

Macie wasn't too excited for a meltdown in the middle of the airport, so she had to do something quick or it would escalate even more. She crouched in front of Ruby and grasped her arms. "You were a *very* good girl on the plane," she said, trying to keep the frustration out of her voice. "And Grandma is going to be so happy to see you that maybe you'll get *two* treats."

Ruby hiccupped. "Two tweets?"

"Yes, two *treats*," Macie emphasized. She let out a slow breath. "Come on. Grandma's waiting, and then we'll get to see the horses, too."

Ruby's watery eyes glimmered. "Can I ride the horsies?"

"Of course," Macie said, relaxing further. Crisis averted. "Now, hold onto my bag while I bring the suitcases."

Ruby sniffled and nodded, then grasped the edge of Macie's bag. It was the best she could do when her hands were otherwise full. Straightening, she balanced the booster seat on top of one of the suitcases, then grasped the handles of both suitcases, grateful they had wheels. She looked toward the exit doors, took two steps, and stopped cold.

Macie recognized him instantly, yet he'd changed, too. Holt Prosper seemed taller than she remembered, his shoulders were broader, and she'd nearly forgotten how his brown hair and blue eyes were so different than his brother's. Granted, Macie had only seen Holt in person three times— their first meeting at the rodeo, her wedding, and the following Christmas season—but how could she have forgotten his square jaw, and those cheekbones that looked like they'd been carved from granite? His light blue button-down shirt only made the blue of his eyes more vibrant, and his faded jeans followed the length of his legs, leaving no doubt that this man was a cowboy through and through.

Her first thought was that she probably looked like she'd been traveling all day with a toddler, and her second thought was why had *he* come? Was Heidi in the car? Macie swallowed down the uncomfortable tightness in her throat that she couldn't quite explain. She knew Holt managed the ranch, so clearly she'd run into him sometime. She just hadn't expected it to be at the airport after narrowly averting a crisis with Ruby.

And now, knowing that Ruby was still on the verge of a meltdown, and would *not* forget the promise to get treats, Macie wished she would have opted for a taxi. Or at the very least spent a couple extra minutes in the bathroom freshening her appearance.

Well, it was too late to check her appearance. Holt was looking straight at them, his expression unreadable. Macie supposed he wouldn't be too happy to have the ranch invaded with guests, but just like Knox always said, Holt was willing to do anything to help his parents out. Even if that meant driving forty minutes to pick up his ex-sister-in-law and her very tired three-year-old.

It had been a sore point for Knox, talking about this family. He had deep resentment against each of his siblings for one reason or another, and Holt seemed to take the brunt of Knox's vicious comments. *He can do no wrong. My parents worship him. They say jump, and he says how high.*

Macie had no siblings, so when she and Knox had gotten married, she'd had the faulty vision that she'd become part of a large family. Two sisters would have been amazing. But things hadn't happened that way. Now, with Macie's mom's death, and not remembering her dad, her daughter's only family ties would be the Prosper family. And as Ruby grew older and asked more and more questions, Macie felt the hollowness that had become their life more acutely.

Every little girl deserved grandparents. And Macie wanted the best for Ruby, even if it came at a great sacrifice on her part.

Like . . . right now.

Walking toward Holt unearthed memories long since buried. Of that hot summer night at the rodeo. How she'd seen Holt casually leaning against the fence, and when her girl-friends caught her ogling him, they'd challenged her to "talk to a real cowboy."

So that's what Macie had done. Then Knox entered the picture and changed her life forever.

Macie blinked away the memory as Holt's gaze went from her, to Ruby, then back to Macie. She forced a casual smile. There was no such return smile on Holt's face. It appeared he was here to complete an errand—which was what she and Ruby would be to him.

Okay, then . . . Macie kept the smile on her face even though her eyes had started to burn. "Hello, Holt," she said when they reached him. "This is my daughter, Ruby."

Holt nodded then dragged his gaze from her face and looked down.

"Ruby, honey, this is your Uncle Holt," Macie said, keeping her tone upbeat.

Ruby's brows drew together as she looked way, way up at the man in front of her. "What's an uncle?"

Hmm. Macie hadn't expected this. "An uncle is a man who is the brother of your dad."

Ruby's nose scrunched. She'd began asking where her daddy was a few weeks ago when she started attending a preschool and the other kids talked about their daddies. Macie had explained over and over that Daddy was working at another rodeo and couldn't come home.

Technically, she and Knox had been separated for over a year, but his family hadn't been told until recently that the divorce was final. Ruby's questions were part of what prompted Macie to call Heidi Prosper, that and her zero balance in her savings account. She'd packed two suitcases, sold whatever else she could, and stored the rest of their belongings at her friend Gilly's place.

"Then where's Daddy?" Ruby asked.

Oh boy. "He's at the rodeo, remember?"

"The doreo is dumb." Ruby's lower lip jutted out.

This was not how Macie envisioned introducing Ruby to her relatives. Time to change tactics. "Can you tell Uncle Holt how old you are?"

Ruby promptly held up four fingers.

"You're four?" Holt said, his voice low.

His voice was deeper than Macie remembered, or maybe it wasn't something that one could recall three years down the road.

Ruby gave a solemn nod. "My birfday's in Duly."

"July," Macie corrected.

Holt kept his blue gaze fixed on Ruby. "So, you'll be five on your birthday?"

A zap of gratitude flashed through Macie. Maybe Holt could diffuse the situation.

Then Ruby frowned. "Four!"

"That's right, you'll be *four* on your birthday, remember?" Macie said.

Ruby's little forehead crinkled further, and Macie bit back a sigh. Arguing with a three-year-old never ended well.

"Then you're the same age as our black pony, Sammy," Holt said.

This changed Ruby's expression in an instant. "Can I ride him?"

He didn't hesitate. "If you can learn the rules."

Ruby was riveted, and Macie was pretty focused as well, wondering what rules Holt could possibly be talking about.

"What rules?" Ruby asked, her eyes going wide.

"Rule number one, listen to your mom," he said.

Holt wasn't even looking at her, but Macie's neck warmed at his reference to her.

Ruby gave an enthusiastic nod.

"Rule number two, learn how to take care of the pony," Holt continued. "Then you can ride him."

"Well, I can do that." Ruby set her hands on her tiny hips.

Macie held back a smile.

"I'll bet you can, little darlin'," Holt said. "You're almost four, after all."

11

Macie knew that they were in Texas, and endearments were a way of speech, so there was no reason for her to tear up when Holt called her daughter *little darlin'*. Just because Ruby had never experienced a father figure in her young memory, didn't mean that Macie had to go all melty around the first male relative to give her daughter some attention. Right now wasn't the time to remember that Knox hadn't seen his daughter in nearly a year.

"We'd better get to the ranch, then," Holt said. "Sammy's getting hungry about now, and I can show you how to feed him."

Ruby looked like a little girl who'd just been told she was a real princess.

Holt lifted the booster from one of the suitcases, then picked up the second suitcase and set off toward the exit, Ruby skipping alongside him.

Macie stared for a few seconds, then realized they were nearly to the exit, and she was still rooted to the ground. She hurried after them, pulling the remaining suitcase with her. Maybe coming to Prosper for the summer had been the right decision after all.

3

HOLT KEPT HIS GAZE on the road as they drove toward the ranch, but it was nearly impossible, because all he wanted to do was study Macie and decide which things had changed about her. Granted, the last time he'd seen her was when she was pregnant with Ruby and sick, so of course Macie had changed. But he had a pretty good memory. Her hair was shorter, falling just past her shoulders, not to her mid-back as before. A detail he probably shouldn't be noticing.

Nor should he notice the vulnerability in her brown eyes. A far cry from when he'd first met her, when she'd been curious and interested, and maybe a bit flirty. And now . . . she had her hands full with a little girl. The moment he walked into the airport, he'd spotted Macie leaving the baggage claim. He could have picked her out in a crowd of dark-haired women, because she still had the same pale pink lips, lithe body, and those long legs.

And she was wearing flimsy, beaded sandals. Something that wouldn't last long if she intended on staying at the ranch for more than a day. Despite his resolve, his gaze strayed to Macie where she sat in the passenger seat. Her pale green print dress set off the honey tone of her skin, along with the several bracelets she wore on each arm. They weren't metal bracelets, but looked woven, with various charms.

Then it dawned on him. Was this the type of jewelry she made? When his mother told him that Macie was in the jewelry business, he hadn't pictured bracelets that looked . . . handcrafted and hippyish. And he hadn't expected her scent of sweet apple to fill the interior of his truck.

"Oh no," Macie said, looking toward the back seat.

"What?" Holt asked, surprised she'd spoken after such a long stretch of silence.

"Ruby's asleep," Macie said. "She's going to be a bear when she wakes up, and then she's going to stay up way too late, and—"

"It's okay," he said. "She's only a little kid. Let her sleep."

Macie bit her lip and glanced at him. "You're right. I get pretty wound up sometimes, I guess. At home, I rely on her napping and sleeping schedule so I can get my own work done."

Holt nodded. "Makes sense, especially if her dad's not around to help."

Macie went silent at that. So . . . maybe don't bring up Knox? Holt had plenty of questions, and he hoped to eventually ask them. First question, *what the hell happened to their marriage?* Second question, *why didn't Ruby seem to know her dad?*

Holt had more questions, about how his brother refused to work any sort of job to support himself or his broken family. Chasing after the rodeo star dream had come at a very high price. And things weren't all peachy at Prosperity Ranch, either. Rodeo events had been steadily declining over the past few years, thanks to a newer generation who preferred to spend their time and money elsewhere. Prosper's own rodeo only had a fraction of tickets sold. Holt could remember when four or five years ago, the rodeo sold out in a matter of days once the tickets went on sale.

A couple more miles passed, and Macie said, "You were really sweet with Ruby. Thanks for that."

Holt didn't want to feel pleased at the comment, but he did. "No problem. I could tell she was giving you a hard time."

"That obvious, huh?" she said in a wry tone. "Do you have any kids, Holt?"

"Me?" The question was logical, but surely, she knew some things about the family. "No, I'm not married." That was probably the worst thing he could have said, because everyone knew that Macie's marriage had been a shotgun wedding. "I mean, I don't have any kids. And I'm not married, either." He really needed to stop talking. "Sorry."

"It's okay." She shrugged. "I know what you mean or *didn't* mean. I'm not proud of everything I've done in my life, but I wouldn't trade Ruby for anything."

He couldn't read her tone of voice. She didn't exactly sound defensive . . . more like *tired.* "Look, Macie—"

"Seriously, Holt," she said. "It's fine. I'm just grateful that you were able to distract Ruby from a full meltdown. I'll tell you, she was close."

"I do have four younger siblings," he said. "So you could say I've seen a thing or two."

The edge of Macie's mouth lifted into a half smile at his comment. And yeah, he'd noticed because he'd slowed to stop at a traffic light and glanced over.

Her voice was much lighter when she said, "What's everyone up to? Your mom told me some basics, but I never had much time to spend on the phone with her. And my calls always had to be when Knox was out of the house, because, well, you know."

Holt did know. He'd never forget the argument between his father and Knox that last Christmas Eve they'd all been together. Knox had said that he had a wife and kid to support and now was the time to make his dream happen. Holt's stomach tightened at the memory, but he didn't want to go there, not right now. So he told Macie about his younger brother Lane, and his two sisters, Evie and Cara.

What he didn't share was that those three siblings were draining the ranch coffers with their tuition and boarding fees. His dad hated dealing with finances, and with his mother's poor health, Holt had been helping out on the personal side. And what he'd found was dismal to say the least. His mother's generosity had left his parents' financial situation in a serious crunch.

Macie asked a bunch of questions, and Holt was once again reminded of all that Knox had taken from their family. Not only himself, but his wife and child—both of whom could have been part of the last four years of family traditions.

As they turned onto the long drive leading up to the ranch, Macie sighed. "Last time I was here, Knox and I left in a hurry."

Holt knew the exact night.

"We drove most of the night," Macie said. "He didn't tell me one word of what had happened until later."

Holt pulled the truck into the circular driveway because he was assuming Macie would want to transport Ruby to a bed and continue her nap. "Look," he said in a low voice, "if I start apologizing for my brother now, we'll be sitting here until the sun sets."

But, oh, did he have questions.

"I don't know what's gotten into me," Macie said, running a hand over her hair. "These memories are hitting me so fast, and . . ." She met his gaze, her brown eyes full of regret. "You don't need to hear all this, anyway."

"I really don't mind," Holt began. "It's only that—"

"Mommy?" a little voice cut in. "Where's the pony?"

Apparently, Ruby's nap was over.

Holt turned to look at her. The little girl's brown eyes, so much like her mom's, blinked back at him. Her cheeks were rosy from her nap.

"Your Uncle Holt will show us the pony," Macie said, "but first we need to unload our things and see Grandma and Grandpa." She cut a glance to Holt.

He nodded. "Remember rule number one?"

Ruby smiled. "I do remember! Listen to Mommy!"

Holt chuckled and opened his truck door. He hadn't planned on enjoying pickup duty today one bit, but he'd changed his mind. His mom needed as much rest as she could get, so Holt had insisted on doing the airport run. Besides, it was good to have Macie one-on-one for a short time, since it gave him a chance to determine where she was at in her life. It would better prepare him for his next conversation with his brother. Holt still wanted to know what had broken up their marriage, besides the obvious selfish traits of his brother.

"Come on, little darlin'." Holt opened the back door, then unbuckled the straps of the booster seat. "Let's get you down."

Macie had opened the door on the other side, and the surprise on her face was clear.

"Thank you for your help," she said in a quiet voice. Next, she moved to the bed of the truck, where he'd stashed the suitcases.

"I'll get those," Holt said. "You'd better keep up with Ruby before she tears through every room."

Macie snapped her gaze toward the house, where, sure enough, Ruby was grabbing the door latch. "Wait for me," Macie called out.

Ruby immediately dropped her hand to her side and looked in Holt's direction, as if to say, *see, I'm listening to my mom.*

Holt nodded his approval, and Ruby grinned.

That kid was precocious, to say the least. Holt unhooked the booster seat, then lifted the suitcases out of the truck. Carrying all three items, he reached the porch, where Macie held the door open with one hand and gripped Ruby's hand with the other.

"It's not polite to go into people's houses without being invited," Macie told Ruby.

"You're both invited." Holt stepped through the open door.

He didn't get very far, because his parents came out of the kitchen. His father, Rex Prosper, had been mayor for nearly fifteen years, and he wore his standard uniform of a pressed button-down shirt, tan Levi's, a thick leather belt with a buckle that read Prosperity Ranch, and boots . . . boots his father polished every day, sometimes twice, if there was an evening event he had to attend.

His father's step slowed at the sight of Macie and Ruby, but his mother rushed forward. She'd dressed up more than she had lately. It was good to see her in a blouse and slacks, versus the robe she wore as she convalesced. She'd also taken time to put on a full face of makeup, making it obvious to Holt she was trying to appear as if she were perfectly healthy.

"Oh my goodness, she's grown so much," his mother said, bending to get a good look at Ruby. "I'm your grandma, sweetie. Do you remember me?"

Ruby gave a solemn nod, although Holt doubted the kid could remember. His mother had been out to see her grandkid a few times, but not for at least a year. And that meant this was his father's first time meeting Ruby. His one and only grand-child.

For now, Rex Prosper stood back, taking in the scene, his gaze moving among the women.

"Can I have a hug?" his mother asked Ruby.

The little girl stepped forward and threw her arms around her grandma's neck. Heidi chuckled and squeezed tight.

Something in Holt's heart twisted. He couldn't exactly explain how he felt both pain and joy at seeing the reunion. Pain because of his brother's choices, and so much lost time, and joy that somehow Macie had made it to Prosper anyway. At this moment, things like his parents' personal debt, Knox's constant requests for money, and Holt's inconvenience at Macie's arrival didn't seem to matter as much as they had only moments before.

Then, his father stepped forward.

"Ruby, this is Grandpa Prosper," Macie said.

Ruby released her grandma and looked at her grandpa. "You're the dayor!"

The grin that broke out on his father's face sent another twist through Holt's heart.

"That's right, sweet pea, I'm the mayor."

His mother laughed, and Macie smiled.

Holt couldn't help smiling, too.

Then Ruby did something extraordinary. She moved to her grandpa and wrapped her arms about his legs. Rex Prosper didn't react for a moment, then he bent and kissed the top of her head. "Welcome to Prosper, sweet pea."

The lump growing in Holt's throat propelled him to pick up the two suitcases and walk past the group. He headed down the hallway to Cara's bedroom, where his mother said she'd put Macie and Ruby. The emotions in the front room were messing with his heart.

As he set the suitcases down and looked around the room decorated in sunshine yellow and white, he knew that with the arrival of Macie and Ruby at Prosperity Ranch, none of their lives would ever be the same. Especially his.

"ARE THESE BRACELETS FROM your company?" Heidi Prosper asked, touching the row of bracelets on Macie's arm.

Macie sat at the scrubbed oak table across from Heidi. Rex had taken Ruby outside to show her about the ranch, and had promised to end up at the barn to take her on her first ride on Sammy, the pony. Macie couldn't have dreamed up a better welcome for her little girl. Ruby was in absolute heaven, and Macie was regretting not reaching out to the family sooner, or even during her marriage to Knox. She should have insisted that he make things good with his dad.

Though she wished she could go back and change things, she knew that it would have been impossible. Knox hadn't even wanted his father's name mentioned. His mother got away with short visits, but those came to an end a year ago when everything fell apart.

"Yes, I guess I'm a walking billboard." Macie looked down at her arm. "I've ordered my next round of supplies to be delivered to this address so I can keep up with my orders. I hope you don't mind."

"Of course not, dear," Heidi said with a smile. "I'm so looking forward to your stay. I want you to feel at home."

"Thank you." Macie met Heidi's blue gaze that was similar to Holt's. Heidi wore more makeup than Macie had ever noticed on her before, and it was clear she'd lost about fifteen pounds. "You've been wonderful. You've all been wonderful. Even Holt seems to have worked magic on a very tired little girl."

Heidi nodded, her eyes bright. "Holt's great with kids— just don't tell him I said so."

Macie completely agreed. "I wouldn't dare." She picked up the glass of peach lemonade Heidi had set before her. The cool drink was sweet and delicious.

"Now, tell me what's going on with Knox," Heidi asked.

Just like that, the elephant in the room had been acknowledged.

Macie set down her glass. "I haven't heard from him in a while."

"That's not what I'm asking."

The no-nonsense tone from Heidi was new, and Macie battled with how much of the truth she should tell her former mother-in-law.

"He still loves you, you know," Heidi continued.

Macie's stomach flipped. This was news to her, and even if it were true, Knox's string of women had said otherwise. "Things are very complicated," she said at last. "Knox and I weren't . . . compatible." In addition to having no idea what Knox had told his family, Macie didn't know what Heidi might tell him about this conversation.

"I think I'd prefer to keep the details to myself for now," Macie said at last. "Everything is pretty raw still." *Please can we change the subject,* she wanted to say. Her eyes smarted, and the last thing she wanted to do was cry over Knox in front of his mom.

Heidi's mouth pursed into a thin line, and Macie hated

the coolness she now felt from the woman. Did Macie not have a right to her privacy? Was she really expected to tell her ex-mother-in-law about the night that she had found condoms in Knox's jacket? Condoms that had nothing to do with their marriage because Macie had been on birth control since Ruby was born.

"Now, tell me how your company works," Heidi asked, her tone still not quite warm.

Macie hid a sigh. If Ruby hadn't been so deliriously happy to go outside with her grandpa this morning, Macie would be seriously second-guessing her decision to come here.

But what had she expected? Coming to her ex-husband's childhood home was certainly going to have some sort of emotional impact. Macie just hadn't planned on his mother's animosity.

"I run the business online." Macie pulled out her phone. "I have classic styles, and customers can order custom styles as well. I try to turn the orders around in a few days so that the customers get them within a week." She showed Heidi the website and clicked through some of the options.

Heidi was silent as Macie shifted through the images.

Then, Heidi pointed to a pale green bracelet with several charms. "This one's nice."

Relief flowed through Macie. Maybe bracelets would be a safe topic between them. "That's the serenity bracelet. I can make you one if you want, or any other combination."

Heidi's gaze cut to Macie's, and her voice was reluctant when she said, "Well, if it's not too much trouble."

Macie had seen the spark of interest in the woman's eyes, and this gave her hope. "No trouble. You're the one who's putting me and Ruby up."

With a stiff nod, Heidi said, "You're family."

There was no warmth in her tone, though. Macie took a careful breath. She needed to keep things mellow. "Ruby was so excited to be around her grandparents." Which was mostly true. Ruby hardly remembered her grandparents.

"Ruby reminds me of her father," Heidi said. "Full of life, and the same expressions. Her little nose, and that darling chin." Finally, the woman smiled, but it was for a reason that felt like a dagger to Macie's heart.

And Macie knew for a fact that Ruby looked like her, not Knox. Yeah, there were small things in Ruby that were similar to her dad, but . . .

"You know, Rex and I have gone through a few ups and downs," Heidi said.

Macie wanted to groan. Because she knew where this was going. And she was right.

"Marriage is never easy," Heidi continued, her tone pious.

Macie wanted to grind her teeth.

"*Men* are never easy," Heidi laughed.

It wasn't funny.

"But there's something to be said about being loyal to each other, and never giving up." Heidi picked up a jewelry piece and turned it in the light. "Especially when a child's involved."

We're already divorced, Macie wanted to shout. *And it was for a damn good reason. Your son is an a—*

While Heidi extolled the virtues of overcoming differences in marriage, and even shared a story of a cousin who'd divorced, then remarried her husband for the second time—and how happy they were now due to marriage counseling—Macie thought of the many nights when Knox hadn't come home. She never knew where he was exactly, or when he'd be home, or if he'd bring home money for groceries, or want to go out for a fancy dinner to celebrate a victory. More often than not, he'd come home in the wee hours of the morning, reeking of alcohol and only making it as far as the couch.

On those nights, Macie knew to stay clear of him in the mornings, and usually the rest of the day. He'd be in a foul mood, complaining about everything and everyone. So she'd take little Ruby out for the day, to the park, to wander the grocery store aisles, or push the stroller for miles along the neighborhood roads. By the time she'd return at night, Knox would be gone again.

Ruby was six months old when Macie found lipstick stains on one of Knox's rodeo shirts she was about to wash. Despite the sick knot in her stomach, she ignored it. She'd seen women congratulate him after a win, and well, not after a win, too. The women didn't seem to care whether he was winning or not. They just wanted to hug the handsome cowboy, so the lipstick could be easily explained away.

The next night, she'd taken special care to get Ruby to sleep early. Macie had done her hair, put on the perfume Knox had always said made him crazy, then dressed in something silky. Then she waited, and waited. She'd finally fallen asleep before he came home, but at least he'd climbed into their bed. Macie had taken a deep breath, then snuggled up to him.

"Late night?" she'd whispered, running her hand across his torso.

He'd grunted.

She'd kissed his neck. "I'm glad you're home, babe." She moved her fingers across the stubble of his jaw, remembering a time when they couldn't be apart for more than a few minutes. And now, she wondered if he had that with a woman who wasn't her.

Knox didn't move, didn't react. Maybe he really was tired. He didn't reek of alcohol, so she knew he wasn't drunk.

Macie propped herself up on an elbow and leaned over and kissed him on the mouth.

Knox placed a hand on her shoulder to stop anything else. "Not now. Maybe when you've lost that baby weight."

And then he turned over on his side, away from her.

Minutes later, he was snoring softly, oblivious to her tears trailing down the sides of her face. When he left the next morning, Macie searched every pocket of every pair of pants and every shirt he owned. Found things she didn't want to find. Condoms. A single earring that didn't belong to her. A receipt for dinner for two people. All things that only proved her husband was no longer hers alone.

"You really should try marriage counseling," Heidi said, breaking into Macie's thoughts with a pat on her arm.

Macie blinked. "But . . . we're divorced."

Heidi didn't seem bothered by that fact at all. "It's never too late, dear."

Macie needed a breather. She needed to leave the house. Go for a walk. Or better yet, a long run. She'd used to run . . . before everything.

How would that look, though? Running out of the ranch house like it was on fire?

Instead, she said, "Where can I find the bathroom?"

"Just past the bedroom Holt set your things in," Heidi said. "This ranch house is too old to have bathrooms adjoining the bedrooms."

"No problem." Macie flashed a smile she didn't feel and headed out of the kitchen. She needed a few moments to herself to try to rid herself of the combatting emotions passing through her. She barely noticed or appreciated the beautiful accents throughout the home. A place where Knox had been loved and nurtured by a great family, yet he had no problem ripping theirs apart.

Once in the bathroom, Macie sat on the edge of the porcelain tub and stared down at the blue and white woven rug on the floor. *Things will be okay,* she told herself, blinking back the threatening tears. They had to be. Seeing Ruby hug her grandparents had been the most precious thing she'd ever witnessed. She could put her pride aside and remain at the ranch this summer for Ruby. Heaven knew that her little girl needed it.

And Macie would figure out the rest. She'd amp up her business, start saving again over the next couple of months, then find another place to live with Ruby. Maybe in Texas. If she lived closer to the Prospers, then Ruby would have more access to her grandparents. Eventually, Heidi would reconcile herself to the divorce, right?

Determined to be strong, Macie stood and noticed the glass mirror slightly ajar. Through the crack, she glimpsed a row of prescription bottles. She moved to close the mirror, then hesitated. Slowly, she opened it wider. All of the bottles were labeled with Heidi Prosper's name. All of them with newer dates, filled over the last few months. The names on the bottles were long and technical, and might not make much sense to most people. But Macie knew instantly what these prescriptions were, and what they were intended to do.

Macie felt numb as she read the labels. Anti-nausea, hormone replacements, white blood cell stimulators . . . they all added up to one conclusion: Heidi Prosper had cancer.

There was no doubt. Macie had spent the last half of her senior year in high school caring for her mother as she went through treatment for aggressive breast cancer. One year later, the cancer returned, and her mother didn't survive. Macie closed the mirrored door just as Heidi called out, "Don't use the bathroom with a blue rug."

The bathroom was pristine, but it was known that

sharing a bathroom with a chemo patient could introduce new germs to the patient.

After Macie found the second bathroom and composed herself, she returned to the kitchen to see Heidi stirring up a new batch of lemonade. "Thought I'd take some out to the men and little Ruby."

"I'll take it out," Macie said in a falsely bright tone, even though her throat and chest ached. "You've done all the work making it. Plus, I should check that Ruby isn't giving them a hard time."

"All right," Heidi said. "I'll start the chicken for dinner while you're gone."

Macie hesitated. "Save some work for me," she said at last. "I didn't come here for a vacation. Plus, I'd love to learn some new recipes."

After Heidi had poured two tall glasses of lemonade, plus a smaller plastic cup for Ruby, Macie headed outside with the tray. The heat was still palpable, and even if the men were in the shade of the barn, she was sure they were plenty warm.

She crossed the wide, green lawn, headed past a corral that was currently empty, then stepped into a barn that was larger than the entire ranch house. Light spilled down from the roof panels, and at the end of a long row of horse stalls, she saw Rex Prosper with her daughter. Rex was a tall man, like his sons, and his once-brown hair was mostly gray now. He was more built like Holt, whereas Knox was leaner like his mother. Rex's eyes were the same green as Knox's, but there was none of the hardness in them. Macie had only seen kindness.

Ruby stood on a wood crate, holding out a carrot for a black pony.

She giggled when the pony leaned forward and nuzzled the carrot. Ruby lowered the carrot, out of the pony's reach.

"He won't bite you, sweet pea," Rex said. "Hold it a little closer. That's the way."

Macie watched the scene as Ruby inched the carrot closer to the pony's snuffling mouth. When he took a bite, Ruby squealed in delight and yanked the carrot away.

Rex chuckled. "He's a big boy, and you're gonna have to give him more than that."

Macie set off down the row toward Rex and Ruby. She glanced at the other horses on her way. Some of them simply gazed at her, others had a wary look in their eyes. She was the newcomer, the interloper, and although she knew next to nothing about horses, she could respect their stately grace.

"Mommy!" Ruby said as soon as she saw her. "I'm feeding Sammy. Then I'm going to ride him."

"Wonderful." Macie smiled at Ruby. It was a bit harder to smile at Rex now that Macie knew what he must be dealing with: a wife with cancer. Macie wondered if Rex also thought that the divorce was a big mistake, and that Macie should give Knox a second chance.

"Grandma sent out some lemonade for everyone."

"I want some," Ruby said, jumping on the crate.

Macie handed Rex a glass.

"Thank you," he said.

The argument between Rex and Knox was what had stopped Knox from keeping in contact with his family, and Macie hoped to one day get Rex's side of the story. As Knox's wife, she'd supported him and tried to be on his side. But as her marriage continued, Macie came to believe that Rex wasn't to blame for the fallout, not even close. How did Rex feel about his son now, after all these years?

"Stop jumping so you don't spill," she told Ruby before handing over the plastic cup to her daughter.

"Yummy." Ruby grabbed it eagerly and downed half the cup.

"Easy there," Rex said with a chuckle. "I've forgotten how much energy little kids have."

"I'm a big girl," Ruby immediately retorted. "Not a little kid."

"So you are, sweet pea," Rex amended. "You're a very big girl who gets to ride Sammy as soon as he's fed."

Ruby gulped down the rest of her lemonade, then picked up the carrot. "Here, Sammy. Eat!"

Macie hoped that Ruby wouldn't wear out her poor grandparents too fast. "Where's Holt? I have a lemonade for him, too."

"He's around the back, by the practice arena," Rex said.

Macie nodded, then continued through the barn and exited through the wide back doors. She stepped out into the sun again and immediately saw Holt. He was kneeling in the dirt, hammering something against a fence. The fence was part of a full-sized arena. Macie hadn't realized how large this property was, and in every direction it seemed to extend for miles.

She headed toward the pounding, and as she neared, Holt looked up.

"Lemonade?" Macie asked. "Your mom made it."

Holt straightened and took the glass she held out. "Thank you." Then he drank the entire thing down without stopping to breathe.

"Can I get you some more?" Macie tried not to smirk, taking the glass back.

"No, that was perfect." He took his hat off and ran his fingers through his hair, which made it a tumbled mess.

Standing this close to him made Macie only more aware of his size, and the fact that she could see the perspiration on his tanned neck above his open collar. She averted her eyes and swallowed. "Um, can I talk to you for a minute? Privately?"

He leaned against the fence he'd been working on. "Doesn't get much more private than this. Not even the horses are paying attention."

She glanced to the other side of the arena that was in partial shade from the barn, where two unsaddled horsed seemed to be half asleep. "What are they doing?"

"They were dropped off yesterday by one of our rodeo guys," Holt said. "Their owner's stopping by the ranch today to talk price. Both horses have been skittish, and they want me to retrain them."

"You're riding rodeo now?" she asked.

Holt's blue gaze on her didn't move. "Training's not the same thing as riding in a competition."

"Right." She looked away again, because when Holt gazed at her, she felt like he was reading way more into her thoughts than she was prepared to share. "So you pretty much do everything here? From mending fences to training horses?"

"I'm the manager," Holt said. "Jerry—the ranch hand—is out with surgery. So right now, you could say I do everything."

Including picking her up from the airport and calming down three-year-old kids. And apparently, dealing with a mom who had cancer. "What kind of cancer does your mom have?"

Holt exhaled. "She told you?"

"No," Macie said. "I went into the bathroom with the blue rug and saw the prescriptions."

Holt's jaw flexed.

"I didn't *snoop*, if that's what you're thinking," she said. "The cabinet was open, and I know those medications."

His brows pulled together. "How?"

She exhaled. Knox knew her mom died of cancer, but he'd never asked any details, or much of anything about her life. "My mom had breast cancer my senior year in high school. It went into remission, then came back a year later."

Holt stared at her.

"It was just me and my mom," she said, "so I helped her through everything. Like I said, I know those medications your mom's taking."

"What about your dad or other family?"

"My dad left my mom when I was about two years old." She met his gaze. "I don't even think he knows she passed away. What's going on with *your* mother?"

"Wait, your mom died?" Holt asked. "And how soon after that did you go on that trip with your girlfriends and end up in Prosper?"

"About a month." Macie felt reluctant to rehash the past. But in truth, maybe it would help Holt understand that she hadn't always been irresponsible. "My friend Gilly thought it would cheer me up—you know, change of scenery and everything. Gilly has a cousin in San Antonio, and we drove out to hang with them. Heard about the rodeo in Prosper and stopped here first."

Holt lowered his head and exhaled. "Unbelievable," he muttered.

Macie was about to ask him what he was talking about when Holt lifted his head. "Mom's got stage two breast cancer. They think they caught it early enough, but they're still being aggressive. She finished her last round of chemo a few weeks ago."

"I shouldn't have come." Macie felt numb again. "I mean, she's in there making dinner right now, and she probably washed bedding, and—"

"Stop." Holt grasped her arm. "A few hours ago, I might have agreed with you, but when I saw Ruby hug her, and that smile on her face . . ." His voice faded away. "I hope you'll stay."

The sincerity in his voice only made her wince. Because she was totally intruding into a family that no longer fully belonged to her. She was divorced from their son. She'd caused enough heartache already, and Heidi was hurting in more ways than one. Maybe Macie should have waited a few years, when Ruby was old enough to come on her own.

And now Holt was being nice to her. It was almost too much to take. Was he hoping she'd reconcile with Knox? Repair the broken mess she'd made of the Prosper family? She wished she could confess the truth of her divorce. She wanted someone on her side, someone who knew the real story about her marriage. But looking into Holt's blue eyes told her that telling him the truth would only bring back the pain. And the Prosper family already had their fair share of that.

5

HOLT SAW ABOUT A dozen thoughts pass over Macie's face in a matter of seconds, and he could probably guess at only a few of them. Doubt, worry, fear, confusion, even desperation. He didn't want her to feel any of them. When Knox had first told him that Macie was coming out to the ranch, Holt's reservations had been strong. His feelings had been complicated, and they still were. And on top of it all, his mom's health was so fragile. But he'd never guessed he'd change his mind about Macie's presence at the ranch so completely.

Yet here he was, holding her arm, telling her not to leave the ranch.

"Mom needs the company and distraction," he said, not sure if he was expressing himself right. And not sure if he was convincing himself more than convincing her in order to override the mess of thoughts in his head. "Mom's been wanting to get to know both you and Ruby better for a long time. She hates missing out on Ruby's life. She's the only grandkid, you know."

"I know," Macie said in a quiet voice. The wind stirred around them, and she moved a strand of hair from her face. Her brown eyes were still deep with sorrow.

Holt couldn't get past the fact that Macie had gone through so many life changes at such a young age: losing her mom in a long battle with cancer, then meeting up with Knox . . . and they all knew how that had turned out. Holt was dying to know what had truly happened to their marriage. Knox had been coy, and Macie . . . she seemed too vulnerable to press for information. Besides, was it truly Holt's business?

Macie bit her lip and looked away. "Seeing those prescription bottles brought a lot of memories back."

Holt dropped his hand from her arm, but he moved closer. He had the insane urge to comfort this woman, take her into his arms and hold her. But he knew it would be better to keep his distance. Macie was his brother's ex-wife, and Holt sensed from his conversation with Knox that things might not be completely over between the two. Besides, logic and reason had to rule.

"I told Mom to tell you about the cancer, but she said she would in time," he said in a low voice. "She hasn't told anyone but immediate family. She doesn't want the town to know or to deal with the parade of food and constant questions that would come as a result."

Macie nodded. "I understand. My mom wanted to do everything herself, too. Until I found her collapsed on her bedroom floor one day after school. After that, I did home school until graduation."

Holt tried to imagine Macie as a young, desperate teenager, faced with such a huge burden. He couldn't even comprehend what she must have gone through. "Sounds rough, and I'm sorry," he said. "Must have taken a lot of initiative to homeschool and take care of your mom."

Macie exhaled. "I wasn't always a knocked-up teenager." Her tone was bitter, defensive.

He felt like he'd been jabbed in the stomach. "Hey, that's not what I meant."

"I know." She looked up at him. "It's just that coming back to Prosper is like getting slapped in the face with my past, you know? And your mom . . ." She hesitated and looked down as the wind picked up around them, blowing her hair against her cheek.

Before Holt could think about what he was doing, he brushed back the strands of hair from her face.

Macie's gaze snapped to his, and Holt knew he had to stop touching her. Now.

He dropped his hand. "What did my mom say?"

Macie really needed to stop biting her lip. The tightening in his gut told him there was only so much he could put up with in one day. And a beautiful, tragic ex-sister-in-law was messing with his mind.

"Your mom's great and all, but I don't think she realizes that Knox and I are legally divorced." Macie took a step back and leaned against the rail. "She wants us to do couple's therapy."

Holt had no words. It was a ridiculous notion, right? Although, he could see where his mom was coming from. Family was everything to her. And he'd heard his parents talking more than once about Knox, and how they hoped that marriage and a baby would keep him grounded. Return him to his roots.

But the frequent calls for money loans to Holt had told him that his brother hadn't really changed. At least not in the ways their parents were hoping he would.

Now, looking at Macie, he wondered if she was still in love with Knox. He'd been her husband, after all. They'd gotten married for a reason—well, more of a reason than pregnancy—because something like attraction and love had got them to that point in the first place. Right? And how was he supposed to answer Macie?

"Do you want to reconcile with Knox?"

"Never." Her reply was swift, decisive.

And it shouldn't have sent a jolt of relief through him, but it did. Then he saw the tears in her eyes. *Damn.* He'd made her cry. Or the conversation about Knox had. Maybe she did want to reconcile, but Knox didn't? Holt was more confused than ever. Whatever the case was, perspiration along his neck was making his skin itch.

"Come in the shade," he said. "It's too hot in the sun."

She walked with him around the arena until they were near the two horses who had the same idea to keep to the shade. He thought of a dozen things to say, how to explain where his mom was coming from, but in truth, he didn't know. His mom hadn't talked much about the divorce, because her life had been consumed with her cancer treatments.

Had Holt missed something entirely? His dad was usually pretty open with his thoughts, and Holt would think that if his mom had been so upset, his dad would have said something. Holt hated to think that his mom was silently suffering. Even more than usual.

But before Holt could attempt to explain anything about his mom to Macie, a deep voice interrupted the quiet.

"There you are."

Holt turned to see Briggs Jones crossing to the arena. He owned the horses that had been dropped off. His farm was on the other side of Prosper, but he didn't have a training facility, or the manpower to do it.

"Your mother said I'd find you back here," Briggs continued, "but who's this?"

Holt had never felt the need to size up Briggs before, yet

suddenly, he was. Briggs was in his mid-thirties, divorced, no kids. He walked with swagger, wearing his usual cowboy hat, but his body had seen better days. And he was looking at Macie like she was a tall, cold glass of lemonade.

"I'm Macie," she said.

"*Macie*, huh?" Briggs said. "Pretty name. You a friend of Holt?"

"I'm his sister-in-law," she said without any hesitation. "I was married to Knox for a while."

Holt decided that Macie was quite talented with putting on a casual face after she had been so upset only moments before.

Briggs's smile widened in the direction of Macie. "Is that so? His loss. Can't say I cared much for Knox anyway. He was a punk of a kid."

"Briggs," Holt said, his tone a warning.

Briggs chuckled. "Well, none of that matters now, does it? How long you in town for, sunshine?"

Was Macie really going to put up with this man's flirting? Apparently, she was. She smiled. "I'll be here all summer. Brought my little girl to visit her grandparents."

"Well, rope me a calf, I'll bet she's as pretty as her mother," Briggs continued. "You'll have to come visit the other side of Prosper. It's where the real cowboys are. None of this fancy ranch stuff."

Holt folded his arms and gave Briggs his best glare.

"These your horses?" Macie asked.

"Sure are." Briggs moved between Macie and Holt and leaned on the fence. "You ride, sunshine?"

"Never been on a horse," Macie said.

Briggs's eyes about popped out. Holt had to admit he was surprised himself. The former wife of a rodeo star hadn't ever been on a horse?

"Well, well," Briggs said with a chuckle. "I can help remedy that."

Macie smiled. "I'll let you know if I need help."

Briggs swept his cowboy hat off his head and gave a mock bow. "At your service anytime, ma'am."

The sight of his sweaty hair and receding hairline didn't do Briggs any service, but to each man his own.

"Did you get my quote?" Holt asked, because it was time to steer this conversation away from Briggs hitting on Macie.

Briggs swung his gaze to Holt. "I did get your quote, and you're asking a steep price. Y'all know that these horses just need a little retraining. They're not first years."

Holt held the man's gaze. Briggs was known for not always paying his debts, and instead bartering on trade. But there was nothing Briggs had that Holt wanted or needed. "I can discount you twenty percent, but that takes us to the line. Can't go lower than that, and we require fifty percent down before training starts."

Briggs rocked back on his cowboy boots as if he were considering the offer. "You drive a hard bargain. Lance charges half your rate."

"Lance doesn't have an arena, so the training is subpar." It irritated Holt to have this conversation at such a basic level. Briggs knew Prosperity Ranch was the best in the entire county, and the prices were fair.

"All right, then, whadd'ya say? Twenty percent off?"

"He said *ten percent* off," Macie cut in.

Both men looked at Macie.

She set her hands on her hips. "Ten percent, or you can load up your horses right now and take them to Lance."

Holt's mouth twitched. She didn't even know who Lance was.

"Your down payment is due by tonight," Macie continued, her gaze steady on Briggs, "or the discount is no longer valid."

Maybe Holt should pull up a chair; it seemed that Macie had this all covered.

Briggs blinked, then he grinned. "I like her, Holt. Didn't know you got a spitfire negotiator employed at Prosperity."

Holt hadn't known that, either.

"Shake on it?" Briggs held out his hand to Macie.

She placed her hand in his, and Briggs's smile widened even more.

"It's a deal, sir," she said. "We'll look forward to that payment and taking good care of your horses."

"Well, I'll be . . ." Briggs said. "And since we're in business together, pretty lady, I'll be obliged if you call me Briggs."

"My pleasure, Briggs," Macie said, that smile of hers announcing her dimple. "You have a nice day now. Holt will keep you updated on the progress of your fine horses."

Briggs smirked, then he laughed. "I've no doubt of that." He tipped his hat, then nodded to Holt. "Good day to y'all."

As Briggs walked away, or strutted away, Holt pulled out his wallet.

"Here," he said to Macie. "You just made me about four hundred dollars, so here's your commission."

She looked at the two hundred dollars in his hand. "Um, no. I'm staying at the house for free. I'm not taking a commission." She moved closer to him and pressed a finger against his chest. "*You* need to stick to your prices, Mr. Ranch Manager. Don't negotiate."

Holt looked down at his chest to where she was touching him. "You think I'm a pushover?"

Her dimple appeared, and she stepped back. "I think you shouldn't let a guy like Briggs tell you what to do."

"Oh really?" Holt held back a smile. "Like *you* are telling me what to do?"

"That's different."

"How's it different?" he asked, taking a step closer.

"It just is."

"Take the commission," he said. "You earned it."

Macie raised her hands and moved another step toward the barn. "No, I'm not taking it."

He moved closer. "I'm serious, Macie. You were brilliant with him, and good things don't go unnoticed on this ranch."

Macie laughed, moving back again. She was nearly to the barn wall. "So you happen to have a wad of cash in your back pocket to dole out commissions?"

"Got paid in cash this morning by another client," he said. "Haven't had time to go to the bank yet."

"I'm still not taking it." She moved against the barn. "Use it for, um, a new hat or something."

"You don't like my hat?"

"It's fine, it's just . . . seen better days."

Holt tried to act offended, but he couldn't stop his laugh. "You shouldn't ever insult a cowboy's hat."

She lifted her hand and tapped the brim, bringing them even closer. "It's a decent hat, but I don't think a new one is going to hurt anything."

He grasped her hand before she could lower it, and his breath slowed. He didn't know what his intentions were, but the warm smoothness of her skin felt nice against his roughened hands. And she still smelled of apple blossoms. Was it perfume? Shampoo? Lotion?

She was staring at him with those large brown eyes of hers, and he knew he was standing way too close. He turned her hand over and pressed the money into it, then he folded her fingers over the money. "Save it for Ruby, then."

He could see the pulse beating at the base of her neck, and he released her hand and dragged his gaze back to her brown eyes.

"Holt," Macie said, her voice strained. "Your dad's calling for you."

He snapped his head toward the barn entrance. Then he heard it.

"We're about ready for you, Holt," his dad hollered from somewhere inside the barn. "Where are you?"

Holt stepped back. Breathed. "Coming!"

Then he strode toward the entrance, afraid to look back. Afraid of what he might see reflected in Macie's eyes. Had she seen through him? Had he given himself away?

6

MACIE WAITED A FEW minutes before following Holt into the barn. She needed a bit of space from him, from the way he'd looked at her, from how close he'd been to her, and from the feel of his callused hand holding hers. If there was one thing a broken marriage had taught Macie, it was the difference between a selfish jerk and a real man.

Holt was one of those real men.

And she needed to stay away from him. Holt was sweet in a way she hadn't expected, especially after all that had happened. She didn't know exactly how she thought he'd act, but it wasn't with kindness and humor. Perhaps Heidi's reaction was the normal one—wanting Macie to give Knox a second chance—and Holt's reaction was the one off base.

His mother's censured words pierced hot through Macie as she remembered the conversation about not giving up on an already dead marriage. *It's never too late. My cousin remarried her husband. You should try marriage counseling.*

She closed her eyes for a moment, blocking out the wide expanse of the ranch, the beauty of the place. *Focus, Macie. Think about Ruby. She's your priority.*

Opening her eyes, Macie headed to the barn entrance. Voices of the men, mixed with Ruby's higher pitched one, brought a smile to Macie's face. Her little girl was loving every minute of this place.

When Macie entered the barn, she was greeted by the sight of Holt crouched beside Ruby, helping her lift a saddle onto the pony.

Rex stood at the head of the pony, keeping the reins in his hands.

Macie didn't want to interrupt anything, but Ruby saw her right away.

"Guess what, Mommy?" Ruby said. "I fed Sammy, and then I brushed him, and now I'm gonna ride him."

Macie smiled at her daughter and walked toward the group. She didn't look at Holt, because she didn't know if she'd cleared all the emotions from her expression yet.

"Good for you, baby," Macie said. She met Rex's gaze, and he winked.

A warm thrill ran through her, as if she'd been awarded something. Approval from her ex-father-in-law? A man she'd never had the chance to get to know. Another confirmation that she'd done the right thing bringing Ruby to the ranch. Macie would just have to figure out how to handle Holt and how to gently let down Heidi.

Holt straightened. "That should do it," he said to Ruby. "Let's get up on the pony now."

The deep rumble of his voice filled the wide space of the barn, and Macie folded her arms as she watched Holt help Ruby onto the pony despite protests of "I'm a big girl," and "I can do it myself."

Macie often wondered if her marriage to Knox hadn't fallen apart, what kind of dad he would have been. Would he have had patience and humor with Ruby, or would he have been easily frustrated?

"I did it!" Ruby shrieked.

Holt didn't even flinch. "What did I tell you about being too loud around the horses?"

"Oh yeah," Ruby whispered loudly. "I forgot."

Rex chuckled. "Let's head out to the corral." He led the pony out of the barn.

Macie followed, and Holt remained in the barn. It was just as well. More space would be good.

When Rex got to the corral, she opened the gate for him, and he led the pony inside. Macie shut the gate, then took out her phone and snapped some pictures. Finally, she leaned against the fence, simply watching Ruby's beaming face as Rex led the pony in small circles.

"Hi, Mommy," Ruby called each time they passed her.

"Hi, Ruby," Macie returned with a smile.

"I don't think she's going to ever get off this thing," Rex said, when he'd passed Macie for the dozenth time.

"I believe you're right," Macie said.

Holt still hadn't come out, and Macie tried not to let her thoughts stray in his direction. He had a lot more to do than entertain Ruby. Besides, Rex was taking care of that.

She looked over her shoulder anyway, but he wasn't at the arena, either, so he must still be inside the barn.

"Hey, Mr. Prosper," she said. "I told Heidi I'd help with dinner. Mind if I head inside?"

"Not a problem," he said. "And please call me Rex."

Macie nodded. "If you need a break from Ruby, just let me know."

Rex grinned and waved her off.

Macie grabbed the empty lemonade glasses, and seeing

no sign of Holt, she walked back to the ranch house, following a path of fruit trees. Prosperity Ranch was like another world, one that she could imagine herself falling in love with. But she didn't have that luxury. As she neared the house, the heaviness in her heart returned as she thought about Heidi and her cancer. Macie hated to think of the woman suffering, and now having to put up with house guests.

Was Macie's presence too much of a painful reminder about Knox as well?

She doubted that he'd repaired his relationship with his dad, and surely that weighed heavily on Heidi. Macie exhaled and smoothed the straying strands of hair from her face. She'd just have to help out as much as possible and hopefully avoid the sticky topic of her and Knox getting back together.

Macie found Heidi in the kitchen peeling potatoes while she sat at the kitchen table. She looked up at Macie with a smile that didn't quite reach her eyes.

"Everyone loved the lemonade." Macie set the empty glasses on the kitchen counter. "What can I help with?"

All the signs of cancer were there: the paleness beneath Heidi's makeup and the weight loss. Macie just hadn't recognized them.

"Oh, I'm nearly done," Heidi said, "and the chicken is already in the oven. You're welcome to go unpack and rest for a while."

Before knowing what Heidi was facing with her health, Macie probably would have taken her up on the offer. But now . . . "How about I set the table and get the water boiling for the potatoes?"

"If you're sure," Heidi said in a hesitant voice.

"I'm more than happy to help and stay busy," Macie said. "Why don't you take a break?"

"All right then," Heidi said. "I wanted to call Knox and

give him an update on your arrival. Not that he'll answer my call, but he listens to my messages."

Macie tried not to cringe in front of Heidi. What if Heidi's message led Knox to contact Macie? She hadn't talked to him for months, and their only communication had been the occasional text. Usually about how he'd be late on child support, again. Macie had long since given up on asking him when he was going to pay. If a check came, then it came. If not, then she made do.

After Heidi left the kitchen, Macie found the pot she needed, then filled it two-thirds full of water and set it to boil on the stove.

Next, she located the dishes, utensils, and napkins, then set a table with five settings. The chair would be too low for Ruby, so Macie found a throw pillow then covered it with a kitchen towel. She'd never cooked for more than a couple of people before, and it was kind of nice to prepare a bigger, fuller meal.

When Heidi returned, her face looked drawn.

Macie didn't know if it was because she wasn't feeling well, or if she hadn't been able to reach Knox. Whatever it was, Heidi was quiet as they worked side by side in the kitchen.

As the minutes passed, Macie grew more tempted to ask Heidi about her health. She had so many questions. But she'd wait. Her very first day at the ranch was probably not great timing.

Macie finished with everything, including chopping veggies for a salad, and Heidi was still peeling potatoes, so Macie found another potato peeler and sat down to help.

"Goodness, you're so thoughtful," Heidi said. "If you're going to do this every day, you're welcome to stay the rest of the year."

Macie only smiled.

"Did you cook for Knox?" Heidi asked.

Perhaps the question was innocent, but Macie couldn't help feeling judged. It would be easy enough for Heidi Prosper to make a long list of Macie's failings as a wife.

"I did when he was around," Macie said. The basics, of course. There was even a span of a few months when she was still pregnant that they'd made friends in their apartment complex and Knox grilled a couple of nights a week. Macie didn't know at the time that those months were the best their relationship would ever be. And even then, things had been unsettled.

"Knox always loved my home cooking," Heidi said in a wistful tone.

Again, the innocent comment pricked at Macie. She only nodded, because it was the best thing to do right now.

"My mother used to say that a well-fed man is a contented man."

Heidi's meaning couldn't have been more clear. Macie's fingers felt numb, and she realized she'd peeled the potato in her hand almost in half. The skin was long gone. She had to change the subject somehow, and fast.

"Speaking of eating, Ruby is finally trying new things," Macie said. "There was a time I either had to bribe or threaten her to eat something other than macaroni and cheese."

Heidi's smile was genuine. "Ruby's a dear, and I'm sure she'll soon learn to eat more things. You've done a nice job with her."

Frankly, Macie was stunned at the compliment. "You're sweet. But I'm afraid that the rose-colored glasses will soon fade. Three-year-olds can be exhausting to say the least."

Heidi clicked her tongue. "Oh, I well remember. I had a house full of young ones at one time."

"How did you do it?" Macie asked. "I mean, on those days that seemed to never end?"

Heidi chuckled, and the sound warmed Macie. Maybe they'd found common ground at last.

"We women all have our secrets," Heidi said.

"Wine?" Macie joked. The second she spoke, she regretted it.

Heidi's pale face flushed. "Wine? No. Nothing like that."

"I'm sorry, I didn't mean—"

Heidi waved her off, but her expression didn't relax. She set the potato peeler down and rose from her chair, then she crossed to one of the kitchen cabinets and opened it.

Macie was surprised to see a row of paperback novels above a row of cookbooks.

Heidi pulled down one of the novels and showed Macie the cover.

"You read mysteries?" Macie asked.

"Yes, I love them." Heidi held the book to her chest. "I mostly read culinary mysteries, and get great recipes to boot. My family loves it when I try new recipes."

Macie rose and crossed to the cupboard and picked up a Mary Higgins Clark book. "My mom loved to read, but I only read when required for homework."

"It's a wonderful escape," Heidi said. "A far cry from ranch work and horses and picking apples. Help yourself to any of my books. Just return them when you're finished. Sometimes, I like to read them more than once."

Macie couldn't imagine how she'd fit reading into everything else going on, but this moment had felt like the first time she was connecting with Heidi. "Okay, I just might," she said.

"Helloooo?" a female voice called through the screen door. "I can smell dinner cooking."

Heidi quickly set the novels back in their places and closed the cupboard. "Barb, is that you?"

"Sure is." The front door opened, and the sound of footsteps approached.

A blonde woman walked into the room. She looked like she'd just stepped off a poster for a rodeo queen and hadn't changed out of her costume yet. Her pink jeans fit her like leggings, and she wore a white and pink glittery plaid shirt. Her blonde hair was huge and curly and must have taken a half bottle of hairspray to keep in place. Her lashes were definitely fake, and her bright blue eye shadow matched her eyes exactly.

Macie couldn't help but stare. Was this woman for real?

"I brought you some early strawberries," the woman said, her gaze landing on Macie. "Briggs told me y'all had visitors, and I thought I'd come introduce myself. Besides, I haven't heard from Holt in a few days, so here I am."

Her smile was so white that Macie wondered if she used white paint on her teeth.

"Barb, this is my daughter-in-law, Macie," Heidi said. "Macie, this is our neighbor and good friend, Barbie."

Barb set the dish of strawberries on the table and waved her manicured hand. "Oh, call me Barb. I haven't been called Barbie since I was a little girl."

"Nice to meet you," Macie said.

"Briggs said you were a pretty lady, and I was a little worried you would steal my Holt away from me," Barb continued with a calculated smile. "But when Briggs said you were the one who Knox married, then I knew I had nothing to worry about."

Heidi scoffed. "You have nothing to worry about, Barb. I know that my son is as slow as molasses, but he couldn't do better than an angel like you."

Barb waved a hand in front of her face as if she were fighting back tears. "Oh, you're too sweet by half, Heidi."

The two women embraced, and Macie felt like she'd entered the movie set of *Stepford Wives*. Maybe it was time for Macie to go check on Ruby again.

"Thanks for the strawberries." Heidi drew away from Barb. "You're always doing something for me, and I can never keep up."

"Well, you've got your hands full," Barb said, her eyes busily taking in every detail of Macie's appearance. "And now, you've got company."

Could her eyebrows lift any higher, Macie wondered? So, Holt had a girlfriend. Good for him. Although Macie wondered why he hadn't mentioned her. And what did Holt see in this Barbie-like woman, besides the obvious physical attributes?

"Sooo, you've got a little girl?" Barb continued, her blue eyes fluttering, and her smile way too perky.

"Ruby's three," Macie said. "She's out with her grandpa riding a pony."

Barb clapped her hands together. "It's hard to believe that the mayor is a gampy. That's so adorable."

Was baby-talking a thing for Barb? "Yes, I suppose—"

"You don't know where I can find Holt, do you?" Barb asked Heidi.

"He's either in the barn or the arena," Heidi said. "Supper's in half an hour, so you should stay. Holt would love it."

"Oh, thank you." Barb brought a hand to her chest. "That's so sweet of you to offer. I think I will. I just love your family." She moved out of the kitchen. "I'll find Holt, then we'll be back in for supper soon."

When Barb left, Heidi smiled over at Macie. "Well, if

you're going to stay all summer, you'll find an instant friend in Barbie. She's as nice as they come."

Macie really wanted to ask more about how serious Holt and Barb were, but she didn't dare. "She seems great," she said at last.

What Heidi said next only made Macie more confused. "Barb's been interested in Holt for as long as I can remember. He's never given much notice until lately. Ever since her engagement to another man in the next town was broken off, Barb's been coming around again. Holt needs to realize that the best woman in the county is right in front of him. He'd better scoop her up before another man does."

Best woman in the county? Macie dreaded meeting the others.

She moved to the cupboards to get dishes and set another place at the table. "Maybe Holt's not ready to commit?" She practically felt Heidi glaring at her back. *Oops.*

"I know that young people today don't really date formally," Heidi said. "But Holt's a grown man."

He certainly was. Macie set down the next place setting.

"I'm sure *you've* dated plenty since your divorce," Heidi said in a huff.

Really? Macie slowly looked up. What she wanted to say and what she actually said were two different things. "Knox was my first boyfriend. And I married him. After we divorced, I decided that Ruby was going to be my main focus."

Heidi folded her arms. "Is that right?"

The woman's tone might be suspicious, but there was a softening around her eyes. "That's right," Macie said. "I don't want to make Ruby's life more complicated than it already is. She doesn't even really understand divorce in the first place."

Heidi was back to pursing her lips.

Why did Macie have to keep defending herself? Time for

a change of topic while waiting for the others to arrive. "Barb looks like she's a regular cowgirl. Does she have a ranch, too?"

"Her daddy runs cows." Two lines between Heidi's brows appeared. The woman wasn't fooled, but she went along with the change of subject. "Barb, well, she's amazing really. Runs half the rodeo now. Always setting up community service events."

Macie didn't doubt it, but she still wondered what Holt truly thought of Barb. She was beautiful in a shiny, glittery, semi-fake way. Holt seemed too down-to-earth for that type of woman.

Heidi pulled out a kitchen chair and sat down. "I think Holt's a bit gun shy after watching what happened between his brother and you."

Macie literally had no answer, and anything she might have said would have come out in a trembling voice. Was Heidi seriously blaming Holt's relationship problems on *her?* Macie turned from the table again and busied herself with stirring the boiling potatoes. She was sure that her face was red from being targeted . . . *again.*

Heidi didn't seem to notice. She continued talking about Holt's dating life. "He was dating someone about a year ago, but it ended, and he wasn't too forthcoming about the reason. But it coincided with your divorce, so it wasn't hard to put two and two together. Those boys are close, you know." She rose from the table and said, "That chicken's smelling done."

Macie stilled. Knox and Holt were *close?* That was news to her. Her mind raced back to recall what all she'd said about Knox to Holt. Would he report back to his brother?

"I can take the chicken out." Macie reached for the kitchen mitts she'd spotted earlier.

Heidi set her hands on her hips. "All right then, if you're sure."

The busier Macie was, the better. "Just tell me where to set the pan so I don't burn your counter tops."

Macie truly didn't know how she endured the next fifteen minutes with Heidi's continued conversation about her sons. By the time the potatoes were cooked, diced, and sprinkled with shredded cheese and fresh herbs, Rex had returned with Ruby.

"Mommy," Ruby called, running into the house.

Macie barely had time to steady herself before her daughter flung her arms about her legs. Sweet relief filled her. A three-year-old was easy to deal with after Heidi Prosper. "Hi, baby, did you have fun on the pony?"

"I love him so much!"

Macie laughed and squeezed Ruby.

Next, Holt came into the kitchen, Barb hanging onto his arm as if she planned to possess the man if it was her dying wish. Was she going to hang on him throughout the entire dinner? It would sure make Macie's first dinner with the Prosper family interesting.

7

DID YOU TRANSFER THE money yet?

Holt glanced at the text that flashed across his cell phone screen where it lay on the kitchen table. He picked up the phone and slipped it into his pocket. Knox would have to wait for his answer, and he wasn't going to like it.

Before Barb had interrupted him, he'd been going over last month's accounts. Things were looking grim; Holt needed ideas to increase the income of the ranch, and fast. If he let things go too long without coming up with a solution, he'd have to let his parents know. As it was, as soon as Holt had everything balanced and the spreadsheets updated, he planned on telling his dad.

Barb was currently leaning close where they sat next to each other at the dinner table. "Lost in thought, pumpkin?"

He gave her a half smile, but tried not to encourage her at the same time.

Barb showing up in time for the family dinner, which his mother served every night at six o'clock sharp, was either completely planned on Barb's part, or a coincidence.

Holt believed it was the former.

Barb was a planner, down to the minute. And when Holt had seen her walk into the office inside the barn, he hid a groan. Barb was relentless. And yeah, she was a nice woman, nice-looking even, but she wouldn't back off.

No matter how politely Holt had turned her down, over and over, she always managed to find him and to somehow work her way into family events that he couldn't get out of. Like dinner.

Walking into the house with Barb clinging to his arm, Holt's first thought was what would Macie think? Which was ridiculous, because who cared what she thought? They hadn't been a part of each other's lives, ever, until today. And now, he was self-conscious about Macie seeing how Barb was hanging all over him?

Macie didn't look at him directly, though, at least not at first. And he couldn't blame her, not really. Things outside had gotten a little too personal for his liking.

"This all looks delicious, honey," his dad had told his mom, kissing her cheek.

"Oh, don't thank me," she said. "Macie did most of the work while I sat at the table and watched."

Macie's eyes did connect with Holt's then. Just for an instant. But in that instant, he understood what she was trying to do: ease his mother's burden. And he was grateful for that.

"Well, pumpkin," Barb had said close to his ear. "I guess we're sitting next to each other."

So Holt and Barb ended up sitting together.

"Will you say grace, honey?" his dad had asked his mom.

His mother smiled. "Of course."

Then everyone grasped hands, and Holt noticed Macie's hesitation. Did she not say grace as a habit?

"Bow your head and close your eyes," his mother told Ruby. The little girl hurried to comply.

Macie took Ruby's hand on one side, and his mother's on the other side of her.

His and Macie's gazes connected again just before his mother began. Everyone else was bowing their heads and closing their eyes. Holt really should have, too, but he couldn't look away from Macie's brown eyes. As it turned out, she closed her eyes first.

When his mother finished saying grace, she continued to talk about Macie's help with dinner.

Barb smiled through it all, then commented, "Macie sure is a good little homemaker. Is there anything you can't do, hon?"

A faint pink had bloomed on Macie's cheeks. "There's plenty I can't do, but I'm willing to learn, especially if it has to do with preparing delicious food."

Holt could practically feel Barb's scowl, although she was still smiling. "How precious."

"Tell us what you've been staying busy with, Barb," his mother said.

If there was ever a favorite topic Barb loved to talk about, it was herself. For the duration of the dinner, Barb spoke about the upcoming rodeo, where she served on the committee, specifically over the barrel racing.

Her voice grew more and more animated as she described her volunteer work in detail, down to the shopping trips she'd planned to get the girls outfitted "pretty as pictures." Holt had no doubt they'd all look like mini-Barbs when she was done with them. That was when Holt had become distracted with the text from Knox and tuned out of the conversation. Barb noticed, of course, if her pout were any indication..

"I'm sorry, Barb," he said. "What were you saying?"

He stole a glance at Macie, who was mostly preoccupied

with cutting up the chicken for Ruby and asking her to eat with her fork, not her fingers.

"I was saying that Macie should come out with me," Barb said, her gaze on Macie.

Macie set down her fork. "Oh, I don't want to intrude."

"No intrusion," Barb said. "Girls' night out is for having fun, getting to know new people, and you're new people. Since you don't have a husband anymore, maybe you'll wanna meet a few fellows, too."

Macie's face was definitely flushed now, and she cut a quick glance at Ruby. "Ruby doesn't get to bed until about eight, and then—"

"Racoons doesn't get hopping until around nine anyway," Barb said. "Small-town bar, and all."

"You should go, Macie," his mother cut in. "Not to meet other fellows, of course, but to become friends with the townsfolk."

Holt stared at his mom. Where was this coming from?

"We'll be home Friday night," his mom continued, "and if Ruby wakes up, we can deal with her."

The hesitation was clear on Macie's face. "I'm not much for socializing," she said at last. "I wouldn't even know where to begin."

"Oh, is your divorce recent?" Barb asked in a hushed voice, although everyone at the table could hear, including Ruby.

Holt cleared his throat, but no one paid him any mind, and Ruby seemed intent on mixing her salad into her potatoes.

"Not recent," Macie said.

Barb's brows rose. "Well, hon, that's what alcohol's for." She slapped a hand over her mouth. "Can I say that word in front of a kid?"

60

That's the least of it, Holt thought. It was becoming increasingly difficult to keep his mouth shut at this dinner table.

Macie's smile was tight. "How about I let you know about Friday later on? See how the rest of the week goes with . . . everything."

"Sure thing, hon," Barb said. "Let me see your phone, and I'll put my number into it."

Macie seemed reluctant to hand over her phone, but she did so. Barb added her number with a flourish.

All Holt could think was that Macie was a brave woman.

"You know, Macie dear, we call it *girls' night out,* but men always happen to show up, too." She winked at Holt. "It's not like we can block them from coming into the bar."

Macie nodded and gave her a faint smile.

Dinner ended not a moment too soon, and it was time for the men to clean up. When Ruby heard that if the women cooked, then men did the dishes, she said, "What about little girls?"

Rex chuckled. "I think there's room right here for a little girl," he said, scooting a chair in front of the sink. "Is there a little girl in here somewhere?"

Ruby giggled and scrambled up on the chair.

Needless to say, Holt got quite wet with Ruby "helping" with the dishes, and truthfully, it was nice to have a break from Barb. But that didn't stop him from worrying about how Macie was handling her blatant questions. When they'd finished, he could hear the women's voices coming from the living room. He'd have to pass by them to get back to the barn. And sure enough, Barb rose to her feet as soon as he headed to the front door and snatched his hat from the coat rack.

"I should be going," she gushed. "Thanks for dinner, Heidi, and it was great to meet you, Macie."

Barb was right behind him as he stepped onto the porch. The sun had set, the fading golden light turned violet, and the night air cooled considerably.

"Have a nice evening, Barb," he told her, putting on his cowboy hat.

Barb gazed up at him and set her hands on her skinny hips. "Well, well, Holt Prosper, you've got your hands full here. What do you say we head on over to Racoons for a night cap? Get some of that worry out of your baby blues?"

"I'm not worried," he said, walking down the steps of the porch.

She scoffed and followed. "You can't fool me, big guy. Having Jerry out means you've got double the work." She touched his arm, sliding her hand up to his shoulder. "Come on, pumpkin, I'm sure you've been working since dawn. Even ranch managers need a break." Her hand didn't move.

She stepped very close, pressing her body against his.

What was she thinking? They were in the front yard, and anyone could look out the windows . . .

Holt hadn't ever made any moves on Barb, and she'd never been this aggressive before. He stepped back. "Have a nice night, Barb. I've got several things to finish before tomorrow."

She let her hand drop as he moved away, but she didn't leave, only watched him. "See you later, pumpkin."

Holt hid his grimace at the nickname she called him. He lifted his hand in a wave, already striding away.

Once he reached the barn, he headed into a section that he'd made into an office of sorts. He'd constructed it for his dad a couple of years ago, but Rex hardly used it, so Holt had taken it over. He pulled out his cell phone and replied back to Knox.

This is the last time, bro. I'm serious.

Seconds later, Knox's reply came. *You won't regret it, stud.*

Sending right now, Holt typed. *It should clear your account sometime tomorrow.*

Beautiful.

Holt set his phone on the desk and logged into the computer. The Wi-Fi from the house barely reached the area. He did the transfer to Knox's account from his personal account. There was no way he could use the ranch funds to do it, even if Knox really did pay him back. Next, Holt pulled up the financial spreadsheet to finish off what he'd been working on before dinner.

Right on the screen, in black and white, was the column for Briggs's horses. The memory of Macie laying down the law with Briggs made Holt's lips quirk. He typed in the amount agreed upon, added a column for "commission," then sent the invoice to Briggs.

His phone buzzed with another text. Holt glanced at the screen. Knox, again.

Speaking of beautiful, how's my girl?

Holt didn't move for a moment. Did his brother mean his ex-wife, or his daughter? Finally, he replied, *Macie and Ruby arrived safe. Ruby rode Sammy today.*

What Holt expected was a warm exchange, maybe some back and forth texting. Instead, Knox wrote, *Figures.*

Holt didn't know how to reply. So in the end, he didn't. And apparently, Knox was done texting for the night. He'd gotten his money, after all.

Holt distracted himself by opening his emails and was about thirty minutes into them when he received an alert from Briggs. He'd paid the down payment.

"Well, I'll be . . ." Holt muttered, leaning back in his chair and scrubbing a hand through his hair. The cheap-as-a-rock cowboy had paid up.

It wasn't until long after dark, long after Ruby would be in bed, and everyone else in the house would be asleep, that Holt decided to head in. Tomorrow, he'd probably move his things to his house in town. With Macie around, Holt didn't need to be so hands-on with his parents.

He exhaled. Exhaustion poked at the edges of his mind. The day had been unexpected, full of information and revelation, and he needed time to process it all.

He walked into the darkened house, trying not to make a sound. After locking the front door, he paused. He thought he'd heard someone in the kitchen.

Maybe one of his parents was still up, getting a drink or something. Hopefully, his mom wasn't sick. A light over the kitchen sink was on—the same light he always remembered being on throughout his childhood.

Holt slowed when he saw Macie sitting at the table, her back to him. She was alone in the dimness, and he didn't know if he should make his presence known.

But before he could head down the hallway, she turned.

"Hey," he said, keeping his voice low.

"You were working this late?" she asked.

He pulled his gaze from the spaghetti-strap tank shirt she wore and what looked like pajama bottoms that exposed a bit of her lower torso.

Holt crossed to the fridge to get something cold—ice cold. "Yeah. I sent some invoices, then wiped out a bunch of emails." He opened the fridge door, and the light spilled out, making him blink against the brightness. "Do you want a drink?" he asked without looking at her.

"No." Her voice was quiet, almost still.

Taking out a water bottle, he closed the fridge before turning around.

She was watching him.

Holt opened the water bottle and drank half of it down. "You're up late."

"It's my only alone time from Ruby," she said. "Normally, I work on my jewelry, but I'm pretty tired—although for some reason, I can't sleep."

Holt leaned against the counter. Sitting at the kitchen table, even across from her, would be too close.

"You've had a big day," he said. "Might take a while to get your mind to shut off."

Macie nodded but didn't respond.

Holt finished off the water bottle, then slipped it into the trash beneath the sink.

Macie suddenly stood from the table, and for a half second, he expected her to say goodnight, then leave. Instead, she walked toward him and stopped next to the sink.

Folding her arms, she faced him. "What was Knox like growing up? I mean, this ranch is amazing. Your parents are hardworking folks. Your family says grace, the men clean up after dinner, your dad is a sweetheart to Ruby, your mom runs herself ragged caring for everyone else when she's battling cancer—" She bit off her words abruptly.

Tears tracked down her cheeks, and everything in Holt's body propelled him forward to take her in his arms. But he couldn't move, couldn't allow himself to react, or he didn't think he'd be able to let her go. Besides, Holt couldn't read what was going on between Macie and Knox. And he didn't think he could ask. Maybe he didn't want to know the truth. Were Macie's tears because she missed Knox?

Holt exhaled, then said in a quiet voice, "Knox was a live wire right from the beginning. As far back as I can remember, he was a daredevil, always with something to prove. Got him a lot of attention, and the more attention he drew, the crazier the stunts."

Macie nodded and wiped at the tears on her face.

"It seemed that all through elementary school, he was grounded more times than he wasn't," Holt continued. "By the time my sisters were born, my mom was busier than ever, and watching over Knox and Lane became my responsibility for the most part."

Macie bit her lip. "That doesn't seem fair to you. You were a kid, too."

Holt shrugged. "Comes with the territory of being the oldest kid of a large family."

"I wouldn't know much about that," she said. "It was just me and my mom as long as I can remember."

"What was she like?" Holt asked, curious, and wanting to steer their conversation away from Knox.

"She was really creative," Macie said. "She ran a tailoring business in our house. I remember I'd go to bed and she'd be up sewing, and when I'd wake up for school, sometimes she'd still be sewing. I don't know how she did it all. Of course, it wasn't until she got cancer that I fully appreciated everything she did for me."

"That's how it is for most of us," Holt said. "We don't appreciate what we have until it's gone."

Macie's eyes flitted over his face, then away. "I don't want to live like that. Not anymore. I want to savor what's right in front of me. Not go chasing after the stuff that doesn't matter, you know?"

In other words, not do what Knox had done. And was currently still doing. Is that what she meant? Or was she regretting her divorce?

Her eyes were back on Holt, and it was both disconcerting and only made him more curious about her. "You're a great mom, Macie."

She turned away then, and he was pretty sure another tear slid down her cheek. He didn't mean to make her sad, or whatever she was feeling. But again, he couldn't exactly comfort her.

"It's been really hard," she whispered. "So, so hard. Yet, amazing and exhilarating, too. I never thought I could love another person so much." She released a slow breath. "She's everything to me."

Holt's body wasn't listening to his brain. He lifted his hand and moved the hair that had fallen over her shoulder. He brushed it back, then let his hand rest on her shoulder for the briefest of moments.

"Ruby's lucky to have you," he said in a low voice.

She closed her eyes, and he slid his hand away. Then, because guilt had reared its head, he stepped back.

"Goodnight, Macie," he said before walking out of the kitchen. He didn't wait for her answer. And maybe she didn't reply. He'd never know.

8

MACIE WAS AWAKE EARLY again for the third morning in a row. The week had both crawled and flown by. At least Ruby was in a decent routine now, and Macie had caught up on the jewelry orders.

A sharp jab in Macie's leg, courtesy of Ruby's kick, reminded her why she was awake so early. Sharing a bed with Ruby wasn't ideal, especially since getting her to sleep in her own bed in San Diego had been a battle. Now they were back to old habits. The sun hadn't even risen yet, although Macie was pretty sure the men in the household were already up for the day, if the sound of showers coming through the pipes was any indication.

Macie had been taking over breakfast preparation duties, which wasn't much, since she wasn't nearly the cook Heidi was. Scrambled eggs and toast was about what she managed. Rex sat down to eat, but Holt was in and out of the kitchen, stopping only long enough to fill a mug with coffee and say, "Good mornin'."

Yet, Macie found she now looked forward to that greeting every day. She knew that Holt was living at his parents' temporarily, and it only made her curious about his place. What his tastes were. She and Knox had never gotten out of the apartment stage, and she'd once dreamed of having a nice home. Being a single mom would likely never get her that.

Heidi Prosper had reminded her of that the day before.

Macie sighed. The woman could be infuriating, yet she was sweet with Ruby, and Ruby already loved her grandma fiercely. Macie would just have to swallow back any retorts about Knox. Heidi still hadn't said a word about her cancer. Macie could respect her decision, but she also wondered if the woman needed someone to talk to.

She climbed out of bed and pulled on a sweatshirt over her tank shirt. Then she made her way to the bathroom directly across from the bedroom. She'd shower later, when the men were out of the house, but for now, she smoothed her hair into a ponytail, brushed her teeth, and washed her face.

Being around men like Holt and Rex was a different experience than being around Knox or his friends. Macie didn't feel like she was being watched or judged. Knox wasn't asking her to get dolled up before his friends came over, and she didn't feel like she was competing with his female friends. At the ranch, she could be herself.

She headed to the kitchen and turned on the coffee machine. Maybe since she was up earlier than usual this morning, she could add hash browns and bacon along with the eggs. She hauled out the sack of potatoes from the pantry and set to peeling them for hash browns. There wasn't much that Heidi didn't make from scratch, so there were no bags of frozen hash browns in the freezer.

Once Macie had a half-dozen potatoes peeled, she grated them into a warming frying pan. Then she got out the bacon from the fridge and started it cooking in a separate pan. Next, she cracked eight eggs and scrambled them up. Heidi usually got up mid-morning, and it would be easy to warm up a plate for her.

Macie paused in her work to gaze out the kitchen window and watch the sun crest the eastern hill on the other side of the arena. The ranch looked like a postcard in the mornings, with various greens, rich earth colors, and painted fences. The beautiful landscape was something to be proud of—no wonder Rex and Heidi loved it. Macie wondered if Holt had always wanted to run the ranch, or if, like Knox, he'd aspired to something else.

Or was Holt truly as Knox had claimed, a puppet to their parents' wishes?

The familiar trudge of cowboy boots on the hardwood floor told her that Holt was coming down the hallway. Yes, she recognized his footsteps now, a little quicker and lighter than his father's. A glance at the clock near the fridge told her he was earlier than usual, too. Maybe he'd have more than his customary coffee?

She busied herself with turning over the bacon, then gave the hash browns a final stir. They were a perfect golden brown now. She switched off the element beneath the pan as Holt walked in. She didn't turn, and he didn't speak.

Without Rex in the room, there was no buffer between them. They hadn't had any private conversations since that first day she'd arrived, when they'd spoken in the dark kitchen. Ruby was almost always with Macie, and Holt was always busy. Which was fine. Fine and good.

"Smells heavenly in here," Holt said.

Macie was so used to his silence in the mornings that his deep voice sent a jolt through her. She stirred the bubbling scrambled eggs, then switched off the element beneath the pan of bacon. "You hungry? Or are you going to stick to coffee this morning?" She hadn't meant to say so much, and she focused on scooping the bacon onto a plate piled with paper towels.

"I don't think I could ever pass up bacon." Holt's voice was much closer now.

Macie hid a smile. For some reason, cooking something that Holt would eat made her absurdly pleased. "Good to know."

Holt was suddenly beside her, and he reached for a piece of bacon, brushing her arm in the process.

Macie raised a brow as he took a bite.

"It's hot," she warned.

He chewed, and Macie probably shouldn't have been staring at his tanned throat as he swallowed.

"Perfect," he said, then winked.

She said nothing as he picked up another piece of bacon, ate that, too, then filled a mug with coffee. She watched his smooth movements, the way that his white shirt was tucked into his jeans, how his boots looked newly polished, and how his brown hair was combed back, brushing against his collar. He seemed more dressed up than usual, sans hat, today.

When his blue eyes connected with hers, she saw amusement in them. Her face heated, which made no sense. It wasn't like she was checking him out . . .

"Got you something yesterday," he said in that low voice of his. "Since you refuse to go into town."

He must have overheard her conversation with Heidi when his mother was going to go grocery shopping. Macie had told her she wasn't ready to face people yet who would ask her questions, about who she was, and why she was here.

But now she was curious. What did Holt get her? He moved to the other end of the kitchen and picked up a sack from the far counter that she hadn't noticed earlier. He set it on the kitchen table, then pulled out two dark red shoeboxes. One large, the other smaller.

She joined him at the table, and he lifted the lid of the larger box and pulled out a pair of deep russet cowboy boots. Women's.

Macie could only stare. They were beautiful.

"I didn't think I could stand seeing you traipsing about the ranch one more day in those flimsy sandals of yours." His gaze moved down the length of her, stopping at her currently bare feet.

Macie took one of the boots. "These are beautiful, Holt. How much do I owe you?"

"Not a penny, darlin'," he said. "Not when you make my parents breakfast every morning."

Darlin'. He'd called her darlin'. She'd heard him use the term plenty of times. With Ruby. Heck, even with those horses he was training for Briggs. To him, it was a common term. So why did she feel like her heart was in her throat?

She focused on examining the boots so that he wouldn't see the emotion in her face. "Well, let's see if they fit, then." Pulling out a chair, she sat and tugged on one of the boots. The interior was soft, and the boot fit perfectly. "How did you know my size?" She looked up to catch his gaze on her legs.

"Uh, Mom went in your room and checked out the sizes of your other shoes." He averted his gaze, and Macie could swear there was more color in his tanned skin than there had been moments ago.

She tugged on the next boot, then stood. Walking around the kitchen, she tested them out. They'd take some getting used to, but they fit fine, and were comfortable. She turned to face Holt, who was watching her, a half smile on his face, his arms folded.

"Will they do?" he asked, his blue eyes searching hers.

"They'll do." She smiled because there was no way to hold it back.

Holt cleared his throat, then pointed to the other box. "Those are for Ruby. She'll probably grow out of them in a couple of months, but I thought she'd like 'em all the same."

Macie crossed to the table and opened the smaller box. The pink boots with a rhinestone buckle twinkled up at her. Exhaling slowly, she pushed back the growing lump in her throat. "She's going to love them." Her voice trembled despite her best willpower not to cry. The tears came anyway. She supposed somewhere in her broken dreams about her marriage, she'd imagined Knox one day bringing home a pair of cowgirl boots for his baby girl.

The man standing across from her didn't have the green eyes of Knox, but blue eyes. He was a man who had more loyalty in one hand than Knox had in his whole body. She stepped toward Holt, and before she could second-guess herself, she slid her arms about his neck.

"Thank you," she whispered against his skin.

Holt didn't move for a second, then his arms came around her and pulled her against him into a full embrace.

"You're welcome, darlin'," he said, his voice rumbling in her ear.

She closed her eyes and pressed her face against his warm neck. He smelled of pine and clean soap, and her heart was beating so hard, she was sure he could hear it.

Macie wanted to melt against him, stay in his arms, continue to breathe him in. Memorize the feel of him pressed against her, the scent of him. How he smelled of soap and pine. But this was oh-so-wrong. Not that she couldn't hug her brother-in-law, but he was her ex-brother-in-law, and he was showing her so many things that were missing in Knox.

Holt relaxed his hold on her bit by bit, and it was a good

thing, too, because Macie didn't have the willpower to release him on her own. Finally, she drew away from him and wiped the tears from her face.

"You okay?" Holt said in a quiet voice, his gaze moving across her face.

"I'm okay," she said. "Sorry about the, um . . . attack on your person."

His lips curved. "I don't mind a hug now and then."

Now Macie was blushing, and she was literally saved by another tread of footsteps coming from the hallway. Seconds later, Rex walked into the kitchen. Macie had made it back to the stove, where she dished up the eggs and hash browns.

Holt had returned to the far counter and located his coffee mug again.

"I thought I was dreaming," Rex said with a broad smile. "Can't tell you the last time I had bacon."

"I guess I'll have to make it more often," Macie said in a bright tone, hoping that her breathlessness wouldn't give her away. "Finally got Holt to have something other than his coffee."

Rex chuckled and glanced over at Holt. "Bacon'll do it. The Prosper men can never turn down bacon."

Macie looked away from Holt before his gaze moved to hers. She felt another blush start, and soon, she'd be bright red. She moved to the fridge and opened the door, pretending to search for something as she let the cold air cool her face and neck—and well, the rest of her body—for a few moments.

Finally, she snagged the pitcher of orange juice and carried it over to the table, where Rex had sat down with his plate piled high.

"Where you off to, Holt?" Rex asked his son.

"Meeting with Steven, remember?" Holt crossed to the

sink and dumped out the rest of his coffee, then rinsed the mug.

He was leaving so soon? Macie moved to the stove to fix her own plate of food.

"That's right," Rex said. "Are you going to give him that discount we talked about?"

"I'm giving him a discount, but not as much as you wanted. We can't afford to budge too much on the price."

Macie sensed he and his father had had this discussion before. She stole a glance at Holt. His tone sounded worried, something she hadn't heard before. Were finances tight? Maybe she should return the two hundred in commission. And how much had those boots been?

"We also need to remember that Steven's brother just died, and he's in over his head," Rex said.

Macie sat at the kitchen table with her plate and poured a half glass of juice.

"Steven is a smart man," Holt said, "and he might have to hire someone sooner than he'd like. But *we* can't be paying the price."

Rex frowned, but he was done arguing.

Before Holt turned away, Macie could see in his eyes, in the tightness of his jaw, that he had more to say. But he wasn't saying it. Was it because she was in the room?

"See y'all later tonight," he said, then paused before leaving the kitchen. "Thanks for breakfast, Macie."

She swallowed. "You're welcome."

Then he was gone.

Rex complimented her on the breakfast, but Macie barely heard him. She was listening to the sound of Holt's truck firing up, then driving away.

9

HOLT DRUMMED HIS FINGERS on the steering wheel as he drove to Steven Pinkney's farm. He had grown used to seeing Macie in the kitchen every morning, and every evening for that matter. This fact alone told him that he'd better get out of the house and off the ranch for the day before he said or did something he might regret.

Macie was vulnerable and beautiful, and she was invading his thoughts way too much. The tilt of her head, the curve of her lips when she was amused, the way she cared for her daughter. The uncertainty in her eyes . . . that's what tugged at his heart the most.

He told himself it was because he was the uncle to her kid. Of course, he was going to care about family. *Protect* family. It was all completely natural and understandable.

The ringing of his cell brought Holt out of his ruminating. Knox's name flashed across the screen. Holt bit back a groan. It was too early for his brother to be awake, which meant that Knox was calling because he needed something.

"Yeah?" Holt answered, hoping that Knox hadn't already blown his way through the last loan.

"Hey, bro," Knox said in a cheerful tone.

Way too cheerful for the crack of dawn. The unease only built inside Holt. "What's up?"

"Just calling with some good news."

"You can pay me back?" Holt blurted.

Knox chuckled. Whatever it was, the guy was in a good mood. "I didn't call to talk money. The news is way better than that."

Holt checked his blind spot then changed lanes. "Spill it, then."

"I'm coming to Prosper," Knox said.

The bottom fell out of Holt's stomach. "You are?"

Knox obviously didn't hear the deadpan tone, and Holt really should be pleased . . . right? Knox coming home after all these years?

"Just registered for the rodeo," Knox said. "It will be like the good ole days. Besides, the ten thousand dollar grand prize looks pretty tempting."

Every word spoken by his brother was like another cut to Holt's skin, because he knew that the coincidence was too great. Knox might say he was coming for the rodeo, but Macie was here . . .

"That prize money is dependent upon the rodeo selling out," Holt said. "Right now, we're not even half-sold. But I'm sure that Mom and Dad will be thrilled to see you."

Knox's tone remained upbeat. "And I'll be right pleased to see them. Besides . . . summer, rodeo, pretty women—what's not to love?"

Holt's stomach roiled. Was Knox going to pick up on women when his ex-wife and kid were in town?

"Of course, there's only one pretty woman I'm interested in," Knox continued.

The conversation was moving forward like a freight train, and there was nothing Holt could to do stop it.

"Macie better watch out," Knox said. "I'm a *new* man, and see if I can't get her back before the rodeo's wrapped up."

Get Macie back? Knox was planning on reconciling? Holt swallowed, his throat dryer than Texan dirt. The rodeo was only a couple of weeks away. "When are you coming out?"

"That's the thing," Knox said. "I'm sort of stuck in Montana with no transportation. Truck's in the shop."

Holt gripped the steering wheel. "What's wrong with the truck?" He bit back a groan as Knox rattled off a few things.

"What's the damage?" Holt asked next.

"Thirteen hundred," Knox said. "But I'm going get some of that knocked off."

Holt exhaled. He was sick of this, but Knox was his brother. And his parents—well, his mother—would be overjoyed to see Knox again. Holt wasn't sure about his dad. But what about Macie? "You really think she'll take you back?"

They both knew who he was talking about.

"I haven't lost my touch, bro," Knox said. "I just lost my focus for a bit. We were married, for heck's sake. And we've got that kid."

Ruby.

"We were young," Knox continued. "I did some stupid stuff. Heck, everyone does, right? Macie's got a good heart. In fact, she's pretty damn near perfect. I don't deserve her, but I've done a lot of deep thinking this past week . . ."

This past *week?*

"And let's just say that the grass isn't always greener on the other side."

Holt wanted to laugh. Or curse. Or hit something. He couldn't think of a way to stop Knox from coming home.

"When are you thinking of coming out?"

"Closer to the rodeo," Knox said. "Got some things to finish up here. Besides, I want it to be a surprise, you know?

Enter the rodeo without Macie knowing, then *boom*. She's watching, and there I am. Like that first night we met. The magic will happen all over again."

Holt wished he'd stuck with coffee at breakfast. His stomach was churning. "The magic, huh? Getting her knocked up? That kind of magic?" Apparently, Holt could be bitter, and he hadn't realized how bitter he was until the words spilled out.

"Whoa, man," Knox said. "Sounds like she's got under your skin. Strutting her little pity party around the ranch, huh? Making me into some big bad wolf like usual?"

"She hasn't said a thing about you," Holt cut in. Well, she had, but that wasn't a conversation he was going to share with his brother.

"That won't last," Knox said. "Why do you think she's out there in the first place?"

Holt could play along. "Why?"

"To get into the good graces of Mom and Dad, of course," Knox said. "She's no fool. Free babysitting. Help with the finances."

Holt clenched his jaw, staring straight ahead. "She's a single mom, Knox."

"Ha." Knox's laugh was bitter. "She's the one who filed for divorce. And the kid *has* a dad. So maybe *I'm* the single dad."

"Not the same thing." Why Holt was arguing with his blockheaded brother, he didn't know. "When's the last time you saw your kid?"

At this, Knox went silent. After a few moments, he said, "I'm not gonna lie, it's been a while."

Holt softened his tone. "That's what I thought." He realized he'd passed the road he'd meant to take. After slowing down his truck, he did a U-turn.

"I miss her," Knox said after a few moments.

Holt wanted out of this conversation, but he had one more question. "You gonna tell me what split you up? The truth?"

Knox sighed. Holt knew that sigh. His brother was about to confess.

"I messed up with another woman."

If Holt had thought he'd been fuming before, it wasn't anything compared to how he felt right now. If he'd been face to face with Knox, Knox would have a bloody nose. "Someone ought to punch you out."

"I know."

And there was no sarcasm in his voice, only remorse.

"I screwed up, bro. Bad," Knox said. "I was a damn fool, and I know I'll be paying for it the rest of my life. But I'm willing to do that. Whatever it takes. I just want Macie back."

Holt pictured Macie's brown eyes, vulnerable, full of pain. And it wasn't just because her marriage had fallen apart, it was because her husband had wounded her deeply. Holt shouldn't be surprised, yet he was. He supposed that he'd wanted his brother to turn his life around so badly that he'd created a fictitious world for Knox.

Macie and the baby would keep Knox honorable. Macie and the baby would create the image of a perfect little family. Knox would come home to his wife and kid at night, and there would be love and laughter. Summer barbeques. First day of kindergarten for Ruby. Another baby on the way.

But that hadn't happened. Knox had ripped out her heart, just as he had everyone else he came in contact with. And what had Macie told Holt the other day? His mom wanted her to reconcile with Knox? Holt hadn't exactly agreed with his mother, but he could see where she'd been coming from.

All of that was out with the trash now. Because that's exactly what his brother was. A piece of sh—

"Holt? You still there?" Knox asked.

"I'm still here," Holt growled. "Someone needs to take you down, and I'm gonna do it if no one else does."

"Hold up," Knox said. "You serious, man?"

"Come on home, and I'll show you how serious I am."

Knox laughed. But it wasn't a friendly laugh. I was more of an *I dare you* laugh. "You're still crushing on my wife, aren't you?" He whistled. "She chose *me*, dude, and she'd still choose me over *you* any day."

Holt really shouldn't be driving. He was going thirty over the speed limit. "I'm going to say this once," he said, slowing and pulling over to the side of the road. "You come home, you're going to tell Mom and Dad what you've done. None of this hero bull crap. You own up to your mistakes, you hear me?"

Knox scoffed. "Always the older brother, aren't you? The boy scout making sure that everyone's doing what they're supposed to. That everything's fair and even. You'd love to see me groveling, wouldn't you? Maybe watch Dad kick me out again?"

"Frankly, I don't care what *you* do on your own," Holt cut in. "But leave the innocent people out of your disgusting habits."

"That's big talk for you, pansy," Knox said. "Have you ever been anything but boring and responsible? Have you ever just lived in the moment? Enjoyed a single day? Saw an opportunity and took it just because you could? Are you even *human*, Holt?"

"I'm human, just like any other guy," Holt spat out. "But that doesn't mean I have to be cruel and selfish."

"Whatever, man," Knox said. "I'm done with the conversation. I'll be there in two weeks, and you can go preach to another choir, 'cause this one ain't listening."

The phone went dead, and Holt chucked his cell across the dash. He released a groan. Knox was coming home. He'd cheated on Macie. Probably more than once. Unbelievable. Holt slammed his palm against the steering wheel, over and over.

Would it be better or worse if Macie knew Knox was coming back? Would she pack up and leave? Or would Holt have to watch the two reconcile?

Don't do it, Macie, he wanted to say. *Don't take Knox back. He'll just break your heart again.*

But Holt knew as well as anyone that he had no right to say anything to her.

Because Knox had been right. Holt was still crushing on her.

10

MACIE'S PHONE BUZZED again right after dinner had been cleared. It was the eighth time Barb had texted her that day. She read the text, which was similar to the previous seven.

Please tell me you changed your mind, hon. The girls are dying to meet you! It will be so fun, and we can drown our sorrows about lame men together. I can tell you all about my ex, too.

Bonding over exes wasn't really Macie's idea of fun, especially with Barb.

Going to a bar and mingling with people who all knew Knox at some point or another, answering questions about herself, and probably Knox as well, didn't sound appealing at all.

Besides, Holt had been gone from the ranch all day. And she felt off, for some reason. She couldn't explain it, but she'd thought Holt would at least be back in time for dinner, and then she could . . . what? Figure out what he thought of their hug that morning? *Nothing,* she told herself. She'd hugged him, and as the gentleman he always was, he'd held her for a couple of moments to comfort her. Because she'd been crying, again, for heaven's sake.

So what if he'd called her *darlin'* a time or two—two times to be exact. She was in Prosper, Texas. Everyone was a darlin', a doll, a sweet pea, even a pumpkin. Which is what Barb called Holt, and Macie could tell he hated it. The thought made her smile.

"Everything all right?" Heidi asked.

Macie looked up from her phone. She'd almost forgotten that she wasn't alone in the kitchen, where she'd spread out her jewelry-making kits.

Rex had snagged Ruby, and they were watching some Disney movie in the other room, so Macie had decided to get a head start on the new orders that had come in that morning.

"Oh, it's just Barb," Macie explained. "She doesn't take no for an answer, it seems."

Heidi smiled. "She's one determined woman. But you'd know all about that, wouldn't you?"

Macie tried not to read into that too much.

"Is this about that girls' night out?" Heidi asked.

"Yeah." Macie set her phone on the table and picked up a small bag of charms. She opened the bag and laid out the charms on a piece of felt so that they wouldn't roll around.

"Ruby will be fine with us," Heidi said. "You should go. Have fun."

Macie wasn't exactly sure why Heidi was so insistent about her going to a bar. Especially when she wanted her to get back together with Knox. "I was speaking the truth when I said that I don't think I'm ready to face so many questions."

Heidi didn't respond, and finally, Macie looked up.

There were tears in the woman's eyes, and Macie felt sick. What had she said?

"What's wrong?" Macie asked.

Heidi brushed at the tears. "I don't know exactly. I'd just

hate for you to cancel on Barb. She's being so sweet to you, and you probably haven't done anything fun for a while."

"That's true, but—" Macie cut in.

"Let me finish." Heidi placed a hand on top of Macie's. "It needs to be said. Yes, Knox took both of you away from us. He didn't want anything to do with our family. But you were our family, too—you and Ruby. And we should have never let Knox stand between us."

"I don't think—" Macie began.

"There's no excuse for our behavior," Heidi said. "I should have gotten on a plane and come to visit more. Rex could have fixed his own breakfast."

Macie smiled, but her nerves were on the rise. Where was Heidi going with this?

Heidi took a shaky breath. "I don't know how I could have five children, and have all of them turn out so different. I'll always love Knox, because that's what a mother does, but I want you to know that *you* are family, Macie. No matter what."

Macie couldn't have been more surprised. And then the real reason came out.

"Besides," Heidi continued, "you'll meet a few men at that bar, and you'll soon realize that maybe Knox isn't so terrible after all."

Macie's breath hitched. "I never said Knox was terrible."

Heidi arched a brow. "Then why did you divorce him?" She lowered her voice. "You can tell me, you know. I can help you better if I know why."

Exhaling, Macie said, "There are some things that will need to stay personal, even if we are family."

"I understand."

Macie tried not to be suspicious. Had Holt talked to his mom or something?

"Holt told us about your mother and how she died," Heidi said. "I'm so very sorry, my dear."

Macie gazed into the blue eyes of the woman who had done a one-eighty in a matter of minutes. Her compassion was undeniable, and Macie regretted the negative thoughts she'd had toward this woman. Heidi had more than her fair share of trials. "Thank you," Macie whispered, because it was all she could manage at the moment.

Heidi clasped her hands together. "Holt also told me that you know . . . about my . . . cancer." Her voice was so faint that Macie wasn't sure if she'd heard her right. "I meant to tell you, but it's hard, you know."

Macie's eyes burned. "I know."

Then Macie moved forward and hugged Heidi. Could life get both harder and sweeter at the same time? Maybe she'd misjudged this woman.

When they drew away, there was a new understanding, a new bond, between the two women. It was as if Macie had the mother that she'd been missing for so many years, and Heidi had healed a small part of the broken heart caused by her son's actions.

"When's your next appointment?" Macie asked. "I want to go with you."

"Oh, you don't have to do that," Heidi protested, though she was smiling through her watery eyes.

"I want to," Macie said. "It would be my honor. I might know a thing or two."

Heidi nodded. "All right, dear. We have a date next Tuesday, then."

"It's a plan." Macie wiped the last of her tears, her heart near to bursting. This was family, she knew. Spending time with Heidi, while her daughter was sitting on her grandpa's lap, in a house full of warmth and concern.

"Go tonight," Heidi said, breaking into the warm buzz surrounding Macie. "Make new friends in Prosper."

Macie exhaled. "I don't know . . ."

Her phone vibrated. Sure enough, another text from Barb. Macie held up her phone with a half-smile. "She's like a pit bull."

Heidi laughed, then Macie laughed, too.

"What does it say?" Heidi asked, her blue eyes bright, as if they were two girlfriends discussing their crushes.

Macie cleared her throat and read, "Checking in again, hon. Still plenty of time to get dolled up. Just come for one hour, and if you don't like it, then I'll bring you home. Promise."

"That's a pretty good offer," Heidi said, her eyes still twinkling. "Hard to pass up."

Macie looked again at the series of texts. Something bubbled inside of her, like anticipation, or excitement? She wasn't sure which. "Okay." She looked at Heidi. "I'll go. But I'll probably be back in an hour."

Heidi grinned. "Good for you, dear. Now . . . what are you going to wear?"

Ninety minutes later, after Ruby had been tucked in more than once, and Macie had finished her hair and makeup in the bathroom, it was nearly time for Barb to pick her up.

Holt still hadn't returned, but Macie couldn't think about that. Why should it matter to her anyway? Neither of his parents had commented much on it, so maybe he was going to spend the night at his own house in town. Maybe he had other things to do. Things outside of Prosperity Ranch. Things that had nothing to do with her.

As she touched up her lip gloss for the third time in the mirror, she wondered who she'd be fixing breakfast for in the morning? Would it include Holt?

"Stop," she muttered to herself. Tonight, she was going out—to a small-town bar, no less. She'd never gone to a bar with friends before. She'd married Knox before she turned twenty-one, and then came the baby.

So it was strange to think this was her first official girls' night out as an adult woman.

She stepped back from the mirror, and although she didn't have a view of her full length, she knew her skinny jeans tucked into the boots Holt bought her looked good. She'd lost her baby weight pretty fast, despite what Knox had said, yet she'd maintained more curves than her younger self. And all the curves were real, unlike the enhanced ones she suspected Barb had. But to each woman her own.

Macie secured a pair of dangling earrings she'd made herself, then she finished curling the last portions of her hair. She wanted to wear it down and wavy, which made her feel more carefree. Younger. Like maybe she could forget her worries for a few hours and have fun.

Or one hour. Whatever.

Her phone buzzed.

In the driveway, come out when you're ready.

She texted Barb. *Coming out now.*

Macie slipped the phone into her back pocket, then opened the bathroom door. The house was quiet. Heidi and Rex must be in their bedroom already. Macie crossed to her room and listened at the door for any sound Ruby might make. Not that Ruby would be quiet if she wanted something.

With a soft smile, Macie walked down the hallway. She opened the front door as quietly as possible. A Cadillac sat idling in the circular driveway.

Barb popped open the passenger door as Macie approached, and three women squealed.

Macie's brows shot up. Apparently, she was the last on the route to be collected.

"Get in, hon," Barb said. "We saved shotgun for you."

Macie slid into the front seat and shut the door. The Caddy pulled forward with a jolt, and Macie fumbled for her seatbelt. One look at Barb told Macie she was way underdressed. Barb wore a dark red cocktail dress that left little to the imagination.

And the two women in the back seat were equally decked out . . .

"Macie, this is Jana and Patsy."

"Hi," both the women said at once.

"And y'all, this is Macie," Barb continued, "the ex-wife of Knox Prosper."

All the women giggled, and Macie didn't know how to react. Did these women know him? And how well? Her face went hot, and she was grateful for the darkness of the night.

"Nice to meet you," Macie said lamely. What did one say to a group of women who were giggling, and about one's ex-husband no less?

"Oh, don't mind them," Barb said. "They've already started their alcohol consumption for the night."

More giggling from the backseat.

Macie stole a glance at the women again. Jana was a redhead with enough makeup on that it looked like she'd bought out the store. Patsy's hair was a short pixie cut. Her eyes were beautiful, almost cat-like.

"What's our bet tonight, ladies?" Barb asked.

"Men," Patsy said.

"Well, duh," Barb said with a scoff. "What about the men?"

Macie looked from Barb to the other women. What were they talking about?

"I bet twenty bucks that Macie will be asked to dance in less than five minutes after we arrive," Patsy said.

"There's dancing at this bar, too?" Macie wasn't prepared for this . . . Was she supposed to dance with a guy on girls' night out?

"Oh, there's all kinds of dancing," Barb crooned. "You name it. Cowboy, line, slow, dirty, and everything in between."

Laughter erupted.

Jana piped up. "I'll bet twenty bucks that Briggs trips when he sees your dress, Barb, and spills his drink straight down his silky shirt."

Laughter filled the interior of the car.

"Briggs wears silky shirts?" Macie asked. When she'd seen him, he was wearing a regular cotton button-down.

Barb snorted. "He does at Racoons."

The women all snickered, and Macie knew she'd have a good-sized headache after tonight with all this laughing and giggling about stuff that was going over her head.

"I'm putting another twenty bucks that there will be more women than men tonight," Patsy said.

"Aw, that's no bet," Barb said. "That's a given."

"Then what's *your* bet, Barb?" Pasty asked.

Barb tapped the steering wheel with a long fingernail. She cast a sideways glance at Macie. "I'm going to put my twenty on Holt Prosper showing up tonight."

The women hooted.

"Did you text him, or something?" Jana asked.

Barb's expression was smug. "No need to. He knows where I'll be."

The women all cackled.

"What about you, hon?" Barb asked Macie through a grin. "We all gotta bet. The money goes into the console between the seats, then the winners get the booty on the way home."

Macie wanted Barb to turn around and take her right back to Prosperity Ranch. She didn't want to dance with any men, and by the sound of it, half the town would be at the bar.

"How about I bet that one of you will lose your bet tonight?"

The women were all silent, as if unsure if her bet was valid.

Then Barb slapped the steering wheel. "It's a deal, ladies. Now let's go stir up this town."

A few minutes later, Barb parked by the curb across the street from a two-story building that Macie remembered seeing the first time she was in Prosper all those years ago.

Barb threw the Cadillac into park with a lurch. "Last chance for lipstick, girls," she announced.

As if on cue, all the women dug out tubes of lipstick and used the interior dome light of the car to apply another layer. Macie made sure her phone was on in case Heidi or Rex had to get ahold of her.

She climbed out of the car with the other women. The street seemed deserted of pedestrians, but trucks and a handful of cars were lined up in front of the bar, and pulsing music could be heard all the way outside. Halfway across the street, Barb suddenly stopped.

"Wait, we need a wardrobe adjustment," Barb said, grasping Macie's arm. "Hang on."

With a swift move, Barb jerked out Macie's tucked-in blouse, undid two of the bottom buttons, then tied the ends of the shirt together. Next she undid a top button. "There, that's much better."

Macie was so stunned, she didn't even react.

The ladies tittered and headed the rest of the way to the

bar before Macie realized she was still standing in the middle of the empty street.

"You coming, hon?" Barb called back.

Yes, she was coming. *Ready or not.* Macie strode toward the women, who were now laughing about something else. Barb tugged open the door, and the pounding music spilled out. Macie followed the women inside, and the first thing she noticed was that the tavern was a lot bigger inside than it had looked on the outside.

The center of the room opened up into a huge dance floor, overlooked by the second floor. People were on the second level, leaning against the railings. Some were dancing up there, too. Barb grasped her arm and led her through the crowd in a weaving pattern, walking around tables, cowboys, and cowgirls.

Even though the place seemed crowded, Macie felt plenty of eyes on her, assessing, curious. She didn't recognize anyone, and it was hard to make out full features in the dim lighting punctuated by roaming spotlights of various hues.

First stop was the bar, which consisted of a highly-polished counter that ran the length of the room. At least a dozen barstools butted up to the counter, and two bartenders worked behind it, seeming to be busy every second. There weren't four available barstools, so the women all crowded around two, between two men, both of whom seemed delighted by the new company.

"Hello, George," Barb said to the man on the left side. His mustache twitched as he gazed at Barb.

"You're a sight for sore eyes, doll," he said.

Barb grinned.

He wasn't a bad-looking guy, though he wasn't much of a standout either. His belly was a bit paunchy, but his eyes were friendly.

"What brings y'all out tonight?" George continued, his gaze moving from one woman to the next.

"We're here to take a break from our woes," Barb said with a wink.

George laughed. "Well, I think I can help y'all with that." His gaze landed on Macie, and his brows raised. "I don't believe we've met, sugar."

Sugar. It was what Knox had used to call her. Macie tried to not let it bother her.

"This here's Macie," Barb filled in. "She's Knox Prosper's ex-wife."

George's mouth fell open, then he snapped it shut. "Well, I'll be." He stuck his hand out. "I heard the guy got married, but found it hard to believe."

The women all smiled in agreement.

Their conspiratorial smiles did nothing to ease the nerves humming through Macie. What did she expect? People around here didn't seem to have a favorable view of Knox, not that she was surprised.

George's gaze did a slow perusal of Macie. "But here's the living proof. I think that calls for a round of drinks for Macie and her friends. On me." He lifted the beer he was already holding.

The women gushed their thanks, and Macie might have mumbled something. She'd made a mistake coming. Barb would introduce her to everyone as Knox Prosper's ex-wife, and she'd have to listen to returning comments all night. She was more than someone's ex-wife.

She felt a tap on her shoulder, and she turned. A cowboy about her height stood there. He swept the hat off his head to reveal cropped red hair. "If this dance isn't spoken for, ma'am, may I speak for it?"

His breath was minty, almost too strong, like medicine.

"Jonny boy!" George said.

The redhead glanced at George and gave a stiff nod, then he turned his attention back to Macie. "Well?"

Macie had two choices: stay with the ladies and drink, or . . . dance. Her third choice to leave wasn't really an option right now. "Okay."

Barb nudged her forward and said something about one bet already won.

Jonny grasped her hand, and at first, Macie was going to pull away, but then she was glad she didn't, or they would have been separated more than once.

The dance changed from a fast-paced country song to a slow-paced song by the time they reached the edge of the dance floor.

Jonny stopped and turned to her. It appeared they were going to dance right there and then.

"What's your name?" he asked, his minty breath assailing her again.

"Macie," she said. "And you're Jonny?"

"I am."

She nodded, and he said nothing else as they continued to rotate in the circles he was leading her in. Maybe this wouldn't be too bad. Jonny wasn't trying to crowd her space. He wasn't asking her a bunch of questions.

Then she glanced toward the bar entrance just in time to see a tall man walk in. Holt Prosper.

11

HOLT HAD SPENT OVER an hour nursing a single beer at the table he'd snagged in the corner of Racoons. He rarely drank the stuff; that was always Knox's department. In fact, it had been months since Holt had been to this bar. Despite Barb's suggestions that they go dancing together, Holt had always put her off. Since his mom's cancer diagnosis, he'd avoided the bar. Until now.

And he blamed Knox for driving him to these lengths. Heat still simmered through Holt from the conversation earlier in the day. Knox coming to Prosper . . . Holt couldn't think of a worse scenario or worse timing. He wasn't naïve, and he knew that relationships could be sticky and complicated. What if Macie forgave Knox? What if . . .

Holt tried to keep his glower to a minimum, but it was nearly impossible. A few people had stopped by his table to say hi, but left after only a moment or two. Holt was just that grumpy, it seemed. Not that he hadn't gotten some interested looks. Primarily from Barb, who'd waved at him soon after he entered. He'd nodded, but didn't approach her or the women she was with.

Driving home that night after a long day, he'd spotted Barb's Cadillac, and he had the insane urge to stop. To see if Macie had come with Barb after all.

His question had been answered in the first thirty seconds after stepping inside, when he'd spotted her dancing with Jonny Rush. Jonny was harmless, and Holt should have turned around right then and there and left. But he didn't leave. He supposed he was equal parts curious and equal parts all about torturing himself. His thoughts were like a broken record, spinning with the same question over and over about what Macie would do when Knox showed up.

Holt bit back a groan.

Ever since Macie had hugged him after he'd given her the boots for her and little Ruby, he hadn't been able to get the feel of her body against his out of his mind. Or her scent. Or the way she'd smiled at him as if he'd just single-handedly handed her the moon, then cried over some damn pink boots.

She was vulnerable, and he didn't want any guy in Prosper to mess with her. He'd go big brother on them if he had to . . . Even as he thought it, he knew his protectiveness over Macie went way above the concerns of any brother, brother-in-law, or ex-in-law. He wouldn't let himself define it right now, though. No. He was at Racoons to unwind after a long day, and an even longer week. Just like every other human inside the place. Right?

And now . . . she was dancing with someone he didn't know—must be from out of town. Maybe a guy here to prep for the upcoming rodeo? Macie looked good in the boots he'd bought her. More than good. Her legs had to be a mile long, and that blouse she wore . . . tied at her stomach and showing more skin than he had a right to notice . . . especially since she was off-limits.

Knox had made that clear.

The way her hair waved down her back and curled against her shoulders only made Holt want to find out if it felt as soft as it looked. She was wearing more makeup than usual, which only emphasized her already naturally beautiful features: her dusty pink lips, those large brown eyes of hers, that dimple.

Knox was an idiot.

Holt took another sip of the now-tepid beer. What did it matter that he was tracking every movement of Macie's? Sizing up every man she danced with? Watching for any signs of distress or burnout? It was because of his careful observations that he saw Briggs before Macie saw him.

The guy wore a patterned green silk shirt. On any other night, Holt might have razzed the guy over his wardrobe choice, but he didn't feel like joking around with anyone tonight. Especially while watching Briggs watching Macie.

Briggs's gaze was locked tight on Macie as she danced with George Anderson.

George was one of those friendly-to-everyone guys; he wouldn't harm a fly. George had also had a thing for Barb as long as Holt could remember, but all Barb did was tease the poor guy by flirting with other men in front of him.

Speaking of Barb, she'd been watching Holt plenty, but had yet to come over. It seemed she was enjoying her girls' night out, while surrounded by half the population of Prosper. Holt shook his head. Barb was incorrigible, to say the least.

Holt's grip tightened on his beer bottle as Briggs reached Macie, interrupting the dance with George.

George didn't seem to mind though—he was just that type of mild-mannered guy. Seconds later, Holt wasn't sure exactly how it all happened, but Briggs was dancing with Macie, and George was sauntering off.

Holt stared.

Macie seemed to be fine, though. She smiled her pretty smile at Briggs, and he laughed at something—that he'd said or she'd said? They danced more to the center of the dance floor, and Holt's view was obstructed by other dancing couples. He tried to relax, but he was more on edge than ever. What could go wrong, though? They were in the middle of the dance floor, and although Briggs hadn't shied away from his interest in Macie, the guy had no record or anything.

Still, Holt stood from the table, trying to get another view.

Ah. There they were. Still dancing. Macie smiling. Briggs beaming.

Holt swallowed the last of his beer with a grimace. Cold beer was decent on occasion, but tepid beer, not so much. He should go. Tomorrow was another early morning, like so many mornings before. Story of his life. Responsible, boring, just like Knox had accused.

Holt headed toward the exit, resolved to let Macie live her life. Enjoy a night out. She was a grown woman. She could handle Racoons.

Just before he left, he glanced over his shoulder. The song had changed again, and Macie and Briggs stood at the edge of the dance floor now. They were done dancing. Even better news for Holt. But then he saw Briggs grasp Macie's hand and gesture toward the exit.

Holt moved aside to let a rather drunk couple pass. His gaze was transfixed on Briggs, whose conversation seemed animated as he gestured. Macie shook her head and tugged her hand away.

Good for her, Holt mused; she could hold her own. Although the back of his neck prickled.

Briggs grabbed her hand again and pulled her close, grinning.

The look of panic that shot through Macie's eyes had Holt striding through the crowd, pushing past people with no apology.

Seconds later, Holt laid his hand on Briggs's shoulder. "Good to see you, man."

Briggs turned, his brows arched in surprise. "Prosper, didn't know you were here."

"I am here." Holt increased his friendly squeeze on Briggs's shoulder. "How y'all doing tonight? Enjoying the music?"

Briggs's eyes narrowed. "Dancing with Macie here, if you don't mind."

"That right? Looks like you were doing something else that wasn't dancing, Briggs."

Briggs tried to shrug off Holt's grip, but to no avail. "What do you want, Prosper?"

"Just socializing." Holt's gaze cut to Macie. She was no longer being manhandled by Briggs, but by the expression in her eyes, she was no fool to what was going on.

She stepped close to Holt and slipped her arm through his. "You promised me a dance, remember?"

Holt stared at her. What was she talking about?

"Come to collect?" Macie asked. "Or are you going to keep on checking out Briggs's nice shirt?"

Briggs smirked. Holt wanted to wipe it off the man's face with his fist.

Macie nudged Holt. "Unless you changed your mind."

Holt swallowed, trying to release the hot anger inside of him. It wasn't even directed toward Briggs. This was all Knox. "I haven't changed my mind."

She smiled, and Holt felt the anger melt from his body. Just like that. His heart did a slow flip.

"Then come on," she said, "time's a wasting."

He released Briggs, who then jerked away. "We're not finished," Holt said in a parting shot before letting Macie lead him to the other side of the dance floor, away from most of the frenzied dancing.

Despite the fast tempo of the music, Macie set her hands on his shoulders as if she wanted to slow dance. Holt had no choice but to slide his hands to her waist. Her exposed skin between the top of her jeans and the hem of her blouse was warm and smooth, and an involuntary shudder sighed through him.

Macie moved even closer, her eyes narrowed. "What was that all about?"

Holt decided to keep the conversation to Briggs. "Was he trying to get you to leave with him?"

"No," she said. "I asked him where he got his shirt, and he wanted me to meet the lady who owns the shop where he bought it. She was sitting on the other side of the bar."

Holt studied her brown eyes. "That's all?"

The scolding in her gaze softened. "That's all." Her fingers played with the edge of his collar, and the brush of her fingertips against his skin sent bits of fire straight to his veins.

Well, then. "You all right, darlin'?" he asked in a low voice.

Her mouth twitched. "I'm all right."

The music shifted then to a slow melody, and the lights dimmed as if on cue.

He should release her. He should walk out of this bar right now.

Have you ever just lived in the moment? His brother's words were like a plague in Holt's brain.

He slid his hands around her back, drawing her close enough so that he could breathe her in. Her body was soft, supple, and he quickly lost himself in her touch, her scent. It was as if they'd been created for this moment, this dance, this . . . Her breathing was as rapid as his. He didn't know what to think about that. She wasn't pulling away or anything. In fact, she'd tightened her hold about his neck and turned her head toward him so that he could feel the warmth of her breath at the base of his neck.

Bumps raced along his skin. "You smell like apple blossoms," he murmured. "Did you know that?"

He felt, rather than saw, her smile.

"Do you like apples, Holt?"

"I love apples, darlin'."

"So if I made you an apple pie, you'd eat it?"

He smiled. "Every last bite."

"Then I guess next time I go grocery-shopping, I'll find some early apples."

He chuckled, if only to cover up a pulse going absolutely wild. Being this close to Macie probably wasn't the smartest thing he'd done that day. Not by far. Besides getting into a pissing match with Knox, the other not-so-smart thing was giving Steven a full discount.

That would be a discussion with his father for later. For now, Holt planned to breathe in the sweet-scented woman he danced with, and enjoy the softness of her hair that kept brushing against his jaw. He'd forget about Knox, and the fact that he'd be showing his cheating face within a matter of weeks.

The song was over much too soon, and when Macie pulled away, Holt felt like he'd awakened from a deep sleep. One in which he was having the most delicious dream.

"Thanks for the dance, Holt Prosper." She tapped the brim of his hat, then she turned and walked away before he could say one word.

She was swallowed up in the crowd before he could come

to his senses and ask her to dance again. Of course, that probably wouldn't be wise. He headed toward the corner table again, only to find it occupied. Well, maybe that was a sign.

"Hey there, pumpkin," a smooth voice said behind him.

He hid a groan and turned around. Sure enough, Barb stood there, her hands on her narrow hips, wearing a flashy red dress that looked like it was two sizes too small.

"Saw you dancing with Macie." Her brows lifted. "Didn't know you were the dancing kind. From what you told me, you hate the bar scene."

Holt really needed another beer, or two. "It's been a long day, Barb, and I can barely remember what I had for breakfast." *Macie's bacon and coffee.* "How about we dance and call it a weekend?"

Barb's face lit up. "Now you're talking, pumpkin." She looped her arm through his, and Holt walked onto the dance floor for the second time that night.

12

MACIE WOKE WITH A splitting headache. She'd had exactly one drink last night, but after getting dropped off by Barb, finding Holt sitting on the porch waiting for her had sure made it hard to fall asleep.

Holt had denied that he was waiting up for her.

Macie had rolled her eyes and moved past him while he held the door open for her. She strode down the hall and went into her bedroom. There was no way she was going to have another late-night conversation with him. Not after that dance they'd shared—a dance that had put her every sense on alert, and some senses she hadn't wanted to admit feeling.

Ruby mumbled something and turned over in her sleep, earning Macie an elbow in the arm in the process.

Macie turned on her side, giving Ruby more room to spread out. Though how much room did a three-year-old really need? It was still early enough in the morning that the sounds of the house were quiet. But if Macie didn't get up soon, she'd be late getting breakfast for the men. Not that they couldn't be on their own for one morning—it was the weekend, after all. But it seemed that the work at the ranch was never done.

She rubbed her forehead, then her temples. She hadn't seen Holt drink more than one beer last night, so he was probably fine. That fact also made her more curious about him. Knox had no problem putting away a six-pack, and more, but according to Barb on the way home, Holt never went to Racoons.

Was there a story there? And why, of all nights, did he show up last night? Macie knew better than to flatter herself that he'd come because of her. Yet, he'd only danced with her and Barb. The rest of the time, he sat by himself. Oh, except for when he nearly punched out Briggs. Macie still couldn't believe how Holt had taken over, all caveman-like. Briggs was harmless. Macie knew his type—flirty—but guys like that moved on almost faster than it took him to introduce himself.

Knox had a few friends like that. When Macie had complained to Knox that his friends were flirting with her, he'd told her to chill out. Yet, when Briggs had been talking to her, the look in Holt's eyes had been anything but chill. Macie wondered what might have happened if she hadn't distracted Holt with a dance.

Macie closed her eyes, and miraculously, she must have fallen back asleep, because the next time she opened her eyes, she could smell breakfast cooking.

What time was it, and did Heidi wake up early? Macie scrambled out of bed, only to notice that Ruby's side was empty. Panic jolted through her, but she firmly told herself to calm down. The house had three other adults in it; surely, Ruby was with one of them. But what if she'd woken up Heidi?

Macie pulled on a T-shirt over her tank shirt, then opened her bedroom door.

The smell of cooking breakfast immediately grew

stronger, and she heard Ruby chattering up a storm in the kitchen. Macie exhaled in relief and crossed the hall to the bathroom, where she quickly made herself half-decent.

Then she headed down the hall and rounded the corner to the kitchen.

Ruby stood on a chair in front of the stove next to . . . Holt?

"That's it, little darlin'," his voice rumbled. "You can flip it now, just like I showed you."

Holt Prosper was making pancakes with her little girl.

Macie stared as she watched Ruby use a large spatula to scoop up a half-cooked pancake, then ever so carefully turn it over. Ruby wore her pajamas, along with her pink cowboy boots that Macie had to practically pry off her at night before bed. The uncooked side splattered a bit, and Ruby yelped.

Holt chuckled. "It's okay. Sometimes, they do that."

But Ruby set down the spatula and folded her arms. "I don't wanna broken pancake."

He didn't seem bothered, not in the least. "I love broken pancakes. Can I have that one?"

Ruby's voice held a smile when she said, "Okay. Do you want me to make you another broken pancake?"

He reached for the bowl with batter and poured three perfectly round circles onto the skillet. "How about we make one for your mom?"

Macie's face warmed at Holt's mention of her in such a casual yet thoughtful tone.

"Can it be that one?" Ruby asked, pointing at the closest pancake he'd just poured.

"Of course." Holt grasped her hand and lifted it out of the way. "Remember, we can't get our fingers too close to the skillet."

Ruby nodded, her tangled curls bouncing.

Macie glanced at the kitchen clock. It was nearly nine in the morning, and she was surprised, first, that she'd slept in so long and, second, that Holt was still in the house. *Oh no.* What if he'd stayed in to watch over Ruby while Macie slept?

"Mommy!" Ruby said, turning to see her.

"Hi, baby." Macie crossed to Ruby and kissed the top of her head. She didn't look at Holt, but she could feel his gaze on her, and she could smell his clean-showered scent of soap and pine. "You're making pancakes?"

"Yep!" Ruby grinned. "That one's yours."

Macie smiled. "Looks yummy." Finally, she met Holt's blue gaze. He hadn't shaved this morning, which was unusual, but the scruff on his chin was just as attractive as his clean-shave. Now, her face grew even warmer.

"How'd you sleep?" he asked.

"Great," she said. "Thanks for, uh, watching Ruby. Did she get you up?"

The edge of his mouth lifted. "No, I was in here making breakfast when she ran in and scared me."

Ruby giggled. "I did. I *scared* him. I said, 'Boo!'"

"That is true," Holt said, smiling down at her.

"I didn't know you cooked," Macie said, still captivated by his eyes this morning. They seemed bluer than ever.

"I do a lot of things, darlin'," he said with a wink.

So, the blush was happening. Now.

Ruby set her hands on her hips, looking from one adult to the other. "*She's* not your darlin', *I'm* your darlin'."

Holt blinked, then he grinned and mussed up Ruby's already messy curls. "You're my *little darlin'*—how's that?"

Ruby wrapped her little arms about his waist and squeezed. "Okay, Holt."

He met Macie's gaze over the top of Ruby's head and winked. Macie's heart skipped about three full beats. *No . . .*

this couldn't be happening to her. She couldn't, wouldn't allow it. Having feelings for Holt Prosper was *not* allowed. Now, or ever.

He was Ruby's uncle, that was all. An amazing uncle. And that didn't translate to Macie herself getting all hot and bothered around him. So what if Holt was a good-looking guy on top of all of his other remarkable qualities? There'd been plenty of good-looking men at Racoons last night, although she couldn't think of any at this exact moment.

Ruby released her death-squeeze on Holt and picked up the spatula again. He guided her through flipping the next three pancakes.

"How long have the two of you been at this?" Macie asked, her focus more on Ruby than Holt, because it was better that way.

"Not long," Holt said. "Are you hungry?"

"Actually, I'm starving." And she was. Her headache had also faded for the most part.

Holt reached for a coffee mug and filled it without moving from his position at the stove. He handed the mug to Macie. "Have a seat. You're our guest this morning."

"Yeah," Ruby piped up. "Holt says that we're bringing you breakfast in bed. So go get in bed."

Holt chuckled. "Your mom can sit at the table now that she's awake."

Macie was blushing all over again, and she turned to walk toward the table so that Holt wouldn't notice. She tried to imagine what it would have been like to wake up to Holt peering down at her with those blue eyes.

She sat down and blew the steam from the coffee. She wasn't much of a coffee drinker, but she'd try some now to get rid of the last of her headache. Ruby carried over a plate of three pancakes, then Holt set down syrup and butter.

"Well, thank you, everyone," she said.

Ruby lugged over the pitcher of juice without spilling a drop, and Holt added a jug of milk to the table along with three glasses.

Moments later, Holt and Ruby sat at the table, too, with their own plates of pancakes. Macie tried not to make too big a deal out of it in her mind, but her traitorous thoughts still conjured up the fact that if she'd married a man who wasn't a cheater and compulsive liar, maybe this could have been her life.

Yet, then she wouldn't have Ruby . . . Ruby, who was currently pouring almost a whole bottle of syrup on her pancakes. Macie reached out at the same time Holt grasped the bottle.

"Easy there, little darlin'—you'll go through an entire maple tree that way."

Ruby stabbed her fork into the center of a pancake and tried to lift the whole thing to her mouth.

"Let me cut it for you." Macie picked up a knife and cut the pancakes into small squares.

Ruby took a bite, and despite the small piece, syrup still made its way to her chin. It was a losing battle, and Macie would definitely be bathing Ruby this morning. Still, Macie smoothed Ruby's hair behind her ears so that she wouldn't get too much syrup in her hair.

She felt Holt's gaze on her, and she returned to her pancakes and took her first bite. They were good—surprisingly good.

"These are great, Holt," Macie said. "Thanks again. You're a man of many talents."

He nodded. "Glad you like them."

"Are your parents still asleep?" she asked, wondering why his dad hadn't shown up in the kitchen yet.

"Yes, ma'am. Saturday's a half day unless there's a town event," Holt said. "In a couple of weeks, the rodeo season will start, and our weekends will be swallowed up with that."

"Are you on the committee, too?" Macie asked, wondering how much more involvement he had with Barb.

"I help with a few things," he said. "And Dad oversees it all, of course. Makes appearances, MCs for the rodeo, that sort of thing."

"My dad's in the doreo," Ruby said.

Holt's gaze cut to her. "That's right."

"When do I get to see him?" Ruby asked, looking at Macie, and it was like she'd been pierced in the heart.

"I don't know, baby," she said, because it was the truth. And now Holt got to hear this conversation again. Thankfully, he didn't intervene, although Macie had no idea what else could be said.

"Grandpa says you're getting pretty good on that pony," he said to Ruby.

A deliberate change in subject. *Thank you.*

"Sammy's my best friend," Ruby announced.

Holt smiled. "Horses make the best of friends sometimes."

Macie leaned over and kissed Ruby's cheek. "I'm glad you love riding Sammy." She looked at Holt. "Your dad is sweet to take her every day."

"It's a highlight for him," he said simply.

Gratitude burned through Macie. And that's all it was, she told herself.

"Can I ride Sammy today?" Ruby asked, looking at Holt.

"Sure thing," he said. "And I think it's time your mom learned to ride a horse, too."

13

HOLT MIGHT HAVE LAUGHED at the expression on Macie's face when he offered to teach her to ride a horse, but he could see she was truly surprised.

Ruby had no such hesitation. "Can we ride our horses together?" she asked in an excited tone.

"I don't see a problem with that," he said, picking up his coffee mug, "although you might have to wait for your mom. Since she's a beginner."

Macie was looking rather pale, though, and Holt wondered if he'd presumed too much.

"We'll see," Macie said in a tight voice. "I'd rather watch you ride on Sammy."

"Please, Mommy?" Ruby said. "You already have boots."

Macie's smile was as tight as her voice. "That's true."

Holt wanted to know what was going on in Macie's mind. But he couldn't very well ask her in front of her daughter. He also knew he could sit across the kitchen table from Macie and stare at her all day, but that wouldn't be productive in the least. Despite her lack of fancy makeup or being dressed in regular clothes, he thought she looked beautiful in her sleepy, untamed way. She wore a dark pink T-shirt and short pajama shorts—something he hadn't seen her in before. The shorts only confirmed his previous assessment of her long legs. Beautiful.

He should move on with his morning. Get out of the kitchen, where it was warm and smelled sweet and . . . He stood from the table and began to clear the dishes.

But Macie sidled up to him at the kitchen sink and took the plate he was still holding out of his hand. "You cooked, I'll clean up."

She turned on the water and picked up the scrubber.

Holt stepped away. "All right. Want me to take Ruby out to the barn until you're, uh, dressed?"

"I should get her cleaned up, too."

"Oh yeah." His gaze cut to Ruby, still in her pajamas. Bits of syrup and pancake dusted her chin and cheeks.

"We'll be out soon," Macie said. "But don't count on me for any lessons."

Holt paused. "Not interested?"

"Not really," she said in a quiet voice.

He studied her for a second, but then decided he wasn't going to be nosy. If Macie didn't want to ride a horse, that was fine. There were still plenty of days left in the summer. As he left the kitchen, he found himself whistling on the way to the barn. The morning air was crisp, the trees blooming all around, and he'd loved spending time with Macie and her little girl.

Don't go there, Holt, he told himself as he entered the barn. Ruby was a doll, and Macie was an amazing woman . . . but Knox would be in town soon enough. That would be a game-changer.

Inside the barn, he began his usual routine, albeit three hours later than usual. Jerry should be back in a couple of

114

weeks, and Holt's work load would shift back to more managerial duties and less of the mucking stalls variety. But for now, the hard labor was good for him and the best thing to get Macie off his mind.

At least as much as possible, knowing she was always somewhere on the ranch, along with Ruby.

Holt spent the next hour cleaning stalls, then he moved onto working with Briggs's horses. They were both coming along nicely and weren't as skittish as they'd been. He'd take them to the arena in town in a couple of days and have them run through several routines beneath the imposing stands. The morning grew hot, and Holt felt the perspiration prickle the back of his neck, which was usually his signal to take a water break. Both for him and the horses.

He headed into the barn, grateful to get out of the sun for a bit.

There, his dad was saddling up Sammy with the help of Ruby. She was dressed in a puffy skirt and floral blouse, with, of course, her pink boots.

"Howdy," Ruby said, smiling brightly at him.

Holt slowed his step. "Howdy, little lady."

Ruby giggled. "Grampy told me that cowgirls say *howdy* when they see a cowboy."

"Yes, ma'am," Holt said, tipping his hat. "That's right."

Rex chuckled under his breath as Holt paused to help secure the bridle.

"I think someone's got you wrapped around her little finger," he told his dad. "Aren't you supposed to be at the committee meeting right now?"

"Got pushed until later this afternoon," his dad said. "And I think this sweet pea has all of us wrapped around her little finger."

This Holt couldn't deny.

"Thanks for the pancakes," his dad continued. "What's got into you lately? You've been whistling up a storm, and now you're cooking?"

"I cook plenty," Holt said. "You forget that I've been a homeowner for going on two years."

"I remember." His dad eyed him thoughtfully beneath the brim of his hat. "Is it that Barb woman who's got you all fired up?"

It took Holt a moment to realize what his dad was talking about. "Barb's a nice woman, but she's a little too, uh, overwhelming for me."

His dad nodded, but he continued to study Holt.

And Holt had the common sense to get back to busy. "Gotta get some water, then finish up training."

Rex gave a slow nod. "Sure thing."

Holt continued on his way, feeling his dad's gaze following him until he turned the corner and walked into the office, where he had a mini fridge stashed with cold water bottles.

He wondered where Macie was. Would she be coming out to watch Ruby, or would she avoid the barn all day because of his offer to teach her to ride? Ever since the argument with his brother the day before, Holt felt an urgency to spend time with Macie. Which was ridiculous because Knox was returning to Prosper to woo her back, and Holt had no claim on her whatsoever.

And wouldn't it just be a slow torture to spend more time with her? Which he kicked off himself by making pancakes this morning, lingering in the kitchen, and then offering to teach her to ride a horse.

Apparently, he was terrible at taking his own advice. He pulled out his cell phone and sent a text. He hadn't texted or called her before. There'd been no need. But he'd gotten her number from his mom regardless.

I have an idea. –Holt

A minute, or two, later, her reply came. *What are you up to?*

Come to the arena, and I'll tell you.

No reply for several minutes this time. Then, she wrote: *Give me twenty minutes.*

With his dad and Ruby in the smaller arena, Holt had the barn to himself to saddle up Bonney, his favorite mare. She was several years old and could run like the wind when she needed to, but overall, she was mellow. He slipped a couple of water bottles into a saddle bag, then led Bonney out of the barn.

He told his dad his plans, then headed to the arena with the mare, where he waited for Macie. If anything, he hoped to find out where her feelings stood with Knox. Did she still harbor hope that he'd change and they could reconcile? By the time her twenty minutes were up—not that Holt was counting—he was practically pacing the fence.

When Macie came from around the side of the barn, his mouth went dry. She was wearing low-slung jeans, a black V-neck shirt, and those boots he'd bought her. Her hair was gathered at the nape of her neck, then braided down one side.

He tried to keep his gaze on her face only, but it was impossible.

"Who's this?" Macie asked, slowing when she reached him, her eyes on the mare.

"Her name's Bonney," Holt said. "Wanna say hi?"

At her hesitation, he moved closer to Macie, still holding onto Bonney's reins. He grasped Macie's hand and brought it to the horse's nose. "Let her smell you first and get used to your scent."

Macie did so. "I feel like a kid. I'm not afraid of horses, I just . . . I don't know. I think it has something to do with Knox."

Holt tried not to react, tried not to let his heart hope . . . did this mean that she was completely over her ex? He exhaled slowly. "I was thinking, if you want, I could take you for a ride on Bonney. You sit in front. I'll hold the reins, and you won't have to do anything. Just relax and ride with me." It was a bold offer. One that would take him across a line he probably shouldn't be stepping over.

Macie didn't answer at first. But she was stroking the horse's forehead now, so Holt took that as a good sign.

"That would put us in very close proximity to each other."

Yeah. He knew.

"Or . . . *you* could ride," he said, "and I'd walk, holding onto the reins, of course. We could stay in the small arena."

He heard, rather than saw, Macie exhale. Then she looked over at him. They were standing only a couple of feet apart, and the depth of her brown eyes made him think about things he shouldn't.

"Holt . . . I don't know . . ."

"What don't you know, darlin'?" he asked in a quiet voice.

"Spending one-on-one time with you." She bit her lip.

Warmth buzzed through him, and not from the sun.

"Dancing with you last night . . . was . . ." She didn't finish, and it was making Holt crazy.

He wanted her to say the words. Out loud. That there was something between them—always had been. And she still felt it. Maybe he should back off. Let someone else teach her to ride.

Instead, he swallowed against the dryness of his throat.

"It's only a ride on a horse," he said in the most nonchalant tone he could muster. "To get you comfortable with the height and the movements. I think if you give it a shot, you might want to try on your own another time."

She scanned his face.

With one look, he swore his heart flipped. How did she do that?

"You could even wear my hat," he offered.

Her dimple appeared. "I'm not wearing your hat."

Holt lifted his hat from his head and moved to set it on hers, but she ducked with a laugh. He grabbed her arm and hauled her against him, then set the hat on her head.

She squirmed, but not very convincingly.

Stop touching her. Let her go. His body wouldn't listen to his brain.

"There," he said, patting the hat into place. "You look like a real cowgirl and as pretty as a peach."

Her hand had curled around his bicep, and her body pressed against his was sending his mind into directions it shouldn't be going.

"You're kind of bossy, Holt Prosper," she said, laughter in her voice.

He also wanted to do other bossy types of things. What he really needed was an ice cold drink. Was her breathing as shallow as his? "So, what do you say, darlin'?"

She smiled. Which created another ripple through his chest.

"I think I'll take you up on it." She lifted the hat from her head and set it securely on his.

Holt chuckled. "All right, all right. Have it your way." He turned to the horse and grasped the reins. "Set your left foot here. I'll help you with the rest."

Moments later, he swung up behind Macie. She was

right. They were in very close proximity. And as Holt secured his arms around her to take ahold of the reins, she relaxed against him.

"That's it," he murmured, then flicked the reins to set Bonney into action.

They moved at a canter at first, and the horse's movements below were rhythmic and steady.

"What do you think?" he asked.

"Not too bad," Macie said. "Can she go a little faster?"

Holt laughed, then clicked his tongue. Bonney sped up. "I think you're catching on."

Macie relaxed further against him, and her braid tickled his neck.

"Where are we going?" she asked.

"To Bonney's favorite stream," he said. "It's not too far, and it will be her reward for carrying an extra load."

"Oh, are we too heavy for her?" Macie asked.

"Not necessarily," Holt said. "She just needs to get used to the weight distribution. You weigh next to nothing."

Macie scoffed. "I'm not the woman I used to be. Having Ruby did all kinds of crazy things to my body. None of which Knox cared for."

Holt tightened his hands on the reins. He wasn't sure what to make of Macie's comment, but if it was what he thought she meant, it was another thing to add to his long list of grievances against his brother.

"I think every man at Racoons had his eyes on you last night," he said at last.

Macie shrugged. "I was the new girl, that's all."

With her back pressed to his chest, and his resolve not to rest his hands on the curve of her hips, Holt felt he had to say at least one thing. "You're a beautiful and remarkable woman,

Macie," he said quietly against her ear. "Any man would be a fool to make you feel less than what you are."

She released a slow sigh. "Sometimes, I wish you'd been the brother to ask me to the dirt dance, Holt Prosper."

Her words were like a dagger of fire to his gut.

Holt should turn the horse around. Right now. Things just went beyond complicated. He said nothing—he didn't trust his reply. The tension between them was charged, and it probably wasn't a good idea that he was practically holding her in his arms, his mouth only inches away from her neck.

Macie could have no idea how much he wished that he *had* been the brother to ask her to the dance.

The one thing Holt knew was that he needed some physical separation from Macie. He slowed Bonney back into a walk as they neared the stream, his thoughts all over the place.

He halted Bonney next to the stream, then climbed off. After helping Macie down, he stepped away, breathed. The vulnerability in her eyes hurt his heart, and he didn't want to wait another moment before telling her a few things. Even if it hurt both of them to do it.

"If I could go back to that night," he said, folding his arms to keep himself from touching her, "and change one thing, it would be to tell Knox to mind his own business. I should have warned you about my scoundrel of a brother. If I would have known what he'd planned—"

"I don't think he planned things specifically," Macie cut in, stepping toward him. "And I don't blame you for anything, Holt. I didn't know either of you. With all my regrets that night, my biggest one was being impulsive. When all was said and done, I think Knox tried to do the right thing. Deep inside, he wanted to be noble."

Holt swallowed back his protest. Being noble was likely

the furthest thing from his brother's mind. "You're a generous woman, Macie." How far would her generosity go, though, when Knox returned? Holt stepped back again because she was still too close.

"Yet..." Her smile was sad. "He wasn't strong enough to truly change. Being on the road so much, surrounded by his vices, made it nearly impossible for him to act the part of a husband and father." She shrugged. "We were both young."

Holt released a slow breath and eyed her. "I get it. But I have a question to ask... what if he *did* change? And what if he wanted to reconcile?"

She looked away, and the breeze tugged on her braid. "I can't even go there in my mind."

It hadn't really been fair to ask her the question. She had no idea Knox was returning to Prosper, and it wasn't Holt's business to tell her. For all he knew, his brother might change his mind.

But Holt knew he'd never change *his* mind about Macie.

"I want to make him pay for what he did to you," Holt ground out. "I want to break his nose and—"

Macie stepped closer and rested her hand on his bicep. "Holt."

That one word stopped him, that and how her touch sent heat searing through him. Could she not hear the thumping of his heart?

When she lifted her hand and placed a finger on his lips, he went up in flames and could barely think straight. "We can't change the past." She lowered her hand, but her fingers strayed to his shoulder.

"I know." His throat felt raw; his chest burned. "But that's not the only terrible thing I want to do." No, punching out Knox was only the beginning.

Her lips parted. "Maybe it would help if you tell me all

the terrible things you want to do. You know, get them off your chest."

Holt doubted that, but he couldn't take his gaze from her mouth. "I want to . . ." He moved back, away from her touch. He couldn't do this. Not because of Knox, but because it wouldn't be fair to Macie.

She dropped her hand, and her eyes flew to meet his. Had she read his mind?

"We should head back," he rasped. "The others will be wondering where we are. I didn't tell—"

Macie moved forward again. And when she placed a hand on his chest, he could only stare into her brown eyes.

"Holt," she whispered. "Wait."

His pulse soared. She moved her hand up his chest, then to the open collar of his shirt, where she brushed her fingers against his skin. Her touch was light, feather-like, but he had to swallow back the pain of not acting on his desires.

She inched closer. The length of their bodies weren't touching, but he could feel the heat of her all the same. She traced her fingers up his neck, then along his jaw. Her hand continued its path behind his neck, and she lifted up on her toes to whisper in his ear. "What if I told you that I wanted you to kiss me?"

Flames roared through him, and it was everything he could do not to drag her against him, and kiss her until they both couldn't breathe.

"Macie, we can't do this," he whispered.

"Because I used to be married to your brother?"

"Yes . . . No." He breathed. "I can't come between the two of you."

She didn't seem to be listening, because she pressed her mouth against the edge of his jaw. The touch of her mouth on his skin was like being branded with a red hot iron.

123

"Macie . . ." His resolve had all but disappeared.

Her other hand skimmed over his shoulder, then curled on his sleeve. "Do you think that for one minute, we could forget about your brother? Maybe pretend you and I just met?"

He closed his eyes. He wanted this, too, so much. Remembering that first moment she spoke to him at the rodeo that one summer night, the breath rushed from him, and he opened his eyes. Macie was here, so close, and the way she was looking at him . . . "If we could go back in time, do *I* ask you to the dirt dance?"

"No," she murmured. "You don't want to be among the crowds and the dirt. So you give me a ride in your truck and take me to your ranch. The house is dark, but we walk among the trees beneath the moonlight. You show me your beloved horses, and I tell you about my home."

"Then what? Do we ride one of the horses?"

"No," she said in a slow tone. "It's too dark for that, but you take my hand as we lean against the fence and talk about our childhoods."

She brushed her fingers against his, sending his pulse soaring.

"Do I get to kiss you before saying goodbye?" he whispered, linking their fingers.

"Yes." Macie's smile was beautiful, creating a new buzz within him. "But it's a very chaste kiss."

Holt's heart skipped a beat, or three. "On the mouth? I don't think that's possible, darlin'."

"I guess we should find out."

He came undone.

Holt stopped listening to the voice telling him to release her. To return to the ranch. To never touch her again. Instead, he released her hand, then lifted his hands and cradled her face. A smiled curved her lips, and her eyes fluttered shut just before he pressed his mouth against hers.

Macie's lips were warm, and she tasted like apples and honey, and better than any dream he'd ever had. He shouldn't be doing this, that he knew, but it was either kiss her or completely break. Her mouth opened beneath his, welcoming him, and she tugged him closer, her fingers gripping the fabric of his shirt.

Holt's breathing stuttered, and their kissing deepened. Tasting, touching. Every sense he had went into overload. He didn't think he'd notice if a stampede of horses headed straight at them . . . he was too lost in the feel of her curves against the planes of his body, the scent of her hair, the taste of her skin.

When she moved her mouth to his jaw and kissed the side of his neck, he didn't know if he could handle any more sensations. He couldn't get enough of her, and he felt his own desperation mount, because he very well knew this would be their first and last kiss. He was burning up, so he pulled her closer, wanting more. Which he couldn't have.

And when her hands moved down the sides of his torso, anchoring him against her, he knew he had to cool things off. Be better than his brother. Show Macie the respect that she deserved. Be honest with her. Come clean.

"Macie," he murmured against her neck. "I . . . we can't."

He lifted his head from the heaven that was her, and it killed him to think he'd have to release this woman. Her eyes were luminous, her cheeks flushed rose, and her lips swollen. The last thing he wanted to do was hurt her. But if he let this continue, let things grow between them, she'd hate him once Knox returned and begged for forgiveness.

"What's wrong?" she whispered.

Holt swallowed. The vulnerability in her eyes only made what he had to say more difficult. And more necessary. "Knox is coming home."

14

SLOWLY, MACIE DISENTANGLED HERSELF from Holt at his news. Knox was coming to Prosper? After all these years? Why? She turned away from Holt, because she'd just had the most amazing kiss of her life, and she was still burning for the man. She didn't want to let him go, but then he'd delivered this blow.

"Why?" she said in a choked voice. When Holt didn't answer, she looked over at him. "Tell me why."

Holt exhaled, then shoved his hands into his pockets and lowered his head. "He's entering the rodeo. Wants to win the prize money."

Macie's breath stalled. Sounded like Knox, but he'd sworn up and down that he'd never step foot in Prosper again. "What changed his mind? Has he reconciled with your dad?"

"Not yet, but he plans to." Holt's voice sounded dull, tired.

Macie closed her eyes. Surely, Knox would come around the ranch, then. Ruby would finally see her dad. Then what? Despite all of her criticisms of her ex-husband, she wasn't ready for these new complications. What would she say to him? How would she act? Especially if they were both around his family at the same time?

"I can't be here when he comes," she said. "I can't see him."

Holt exhaled. "Are things really that estranged between the two of you?"

She opened her eyes and gazed at Holt across the space now dividing them. She'd just kissed this man, went through every exhilarating feeling, and now . . . Macie rubbed the sides of her neck with both hands. "Your mom . . . She'll be so happy to see him, and she'll think that we're getting back together."

Holt set his hands on his hips and pressed his lips tight.

"What?" Macie asked.

"He does want to get back together with you."

Macie frowned. "He *told* you that?"

Holt's slow nod was all the confirmation she needed.

"I have to leave the ranch," she said, panic shooting through her. "I mean, he has the right to see his daughter. Our custody is joint, but . . ." Tears started, and she blinked them away.

"Macie, I have to ask you something."

She wiped at her stubborn tears. "Okay."

"Knox says that he's changed and that he aims to win you back," Holt said. "And if you can put everything between *us* behind you, count it as a temporary distraction or something, don't you think getting back together with Knox would be best for you? And Ruby? The family?"

Anger and shame bubbled inside of her. Is this what Holt thought she should do? Accept and forgive and pretend that Knox hadn't trod on her like the dirt beneath his feet so that the *family* could be happy? What about *her*? And what kind of example would she be to her daughter if she let a man treat her like dirt?

Macie had given him multiple chances. And maybe he would change, one day. But it wouldn't be for her.

"Do you think he's truly changed?" Macie asked Holt point blank. "When you last talked to him, did he sound like a changed man?"

Holt's gaze shifted. "I don't know, Macie."

"Tell me the truth. What does your gut tell you, Holt Prosper?"

His blue eyes slid back to hers. "He's borrowed money from me multiple times. I've been able to cover some of it with ranch profits, but those are depleted right now, so the last loan was from my personal savings. So, as far as his usual money issues, that hasn't changed."

Macie lifted her chin. "Did he tell you what he did to me?"

"He said he messed up with a woman, and he's not proud of what he did."

She folded her arms. "It seems that being broke has given him a conscience, but am I the one who has to continually be punished over and over for it? I can't trust him, Holt, and I'm sorry if that offends you or your mother or anyone else in Prosper. Your brother doesn't love me, not really. No man who's in love with his wife would do the things Knox has done to me."

Holt closed the distance between them and gently took ahold of her arms. "What happened between the two of you? He told me he messed up with a woman. Were there more?"

"There were *multiple* women, and I ignored the evidence for too long." Macie said, pulling out of his grasp, because Holt's hands on her were changing her focus. "He went on drinking binges that incapacitated him for days. I never once felt like I could leave him alone with the baby. I was a single mother the moment I became pregnant. Even the early days were laced with *his* agenda, *his* partying, and the constant accolades *he* needed."

Holt stared at her for a long moment. "I'm sorry, Macie. None of us knew—truly knew. I should have come to San Diego and beat the hell out of him."

Another round of tears started. "I wish you would have." She hated that her voice was trembling and her chest was heaving. She'd cried enough tears over Knox, and he didn't deserve any more.

Holt's arms went around her, strong and sure. Macie couldn't help but cling to him. This man had been so good to her, which only brought on another wave of grief for her choices so long ago.

When her tears finally calmed, and she was pretty sure she'd worn Holt out, she said, "Maybe I shouldn't have kissed you, but I want you to know that Knox and I are over. I wouldn't have kissed you if I thought I'd ever get back with him."

Holt drew away and set his hands on her shoulders. "I really want to believe that, Macie. But you might understand my insecurity here . . . I mean, I've watched my brother charm women for years. Even you. *Especially* you."

"You can consider this woman officially uncharmed by Knox," she said.

Holt's gaze searched hers. "I believe you, darlin'. And you need to know that I care for you. More than I should under the circumstances."

She blinked back new tears. "I care about you, too, and not as a brother-in-law, or anything close to that."

The edges of his mouth lifted. "That's good to hear." He lifted his hand, and his thumb traced the edge of her jaw as goose bumps scattered along her skin. Then he lowered his head and leaned his forehead on hers.

Macie closed her eyes. "I still don't want to be here when he comes to Prosper."

"We'll cross that bridge later," Holt's voice rumbled. "But I think we should tell my parents, about *us*, before he shows up."

"No," Macie said, lifting her head. "Not yet. I mean . . . I don't think your mom could take another shock."

Holt studied her for a second. "You're probably right. She's been through a lot. And more time would be good."

"We can sneak away sometimes, right?" she said. "This is a nice getaway place."

Holt chuckled and glanced around, then his gaze landed back on hers, more intense than before. "Yeah. I like having you all to myself."

She slid her hands over his shoulders, then slowly down his arms, over his biceps, her fingers exploring his contours. When her hands shifted to his chest, then lower to his stomach, Holt said, "Macie, you're setting me on fire, darlin'."

She only smiled, and he growled, then tugged her against him and kissed her hard. She liked this side to Holt, so different from his usual calm and decisive manner. Holt undone was sexy, and his hands created his own path of fire along her skin as he deepened and slowed their kissing.

Macie was no longer a teenager star-struck over a rodeo champion. She was a grown woman with a child, and she wasn't to be waylaid by flattering words or false promises. But beneath her hands, the solid warmth of Holt was unlike anything she'd ever experienced, or allowed herself to hope for. Things were beyond complicated between them, yet in this copse of trees, the outside world felt miles away.

But it was time to return to reality; they both knew it.

When Holt released her, he kissed her softly on the

cheek, then he linked their fingers as they walked back to the horse. She liked this—simply holding Holt's hand. And she wondered if there would ever be a time or place they could do this in public.

Holt helped her onto the horse, and after he mounted behind her, he handed her the reins.

"Your turn, darlin'."

"I don't think so."

"Here," he said, his voice rumbling next to her ear as he wrapped his big hands around hers. "It's not hard. I promise. And I'll be right here if you need help."

Macie smiled. It was like he'd spoken the truth about everything in that sentence.

"Okay." She flicked the reins. Miraculously, Bonney began to walk. "She's walking."

Holt chuckled, and his chest vibrated against her back.

"You need to give me a little room," she told Holt, because his arms were fully wrapped around her waist. "Everyone a mile away will know we've been up to something."

"You're probably right," he said, but for several moments, he didn't release her. Not until the barn and arena came into view.

"Holt."

"All right." He set his hands lightly on her hips.

They soon saw the smaller arena where Ruby was on the pony, with Rex holding the reins.

"She's a natural," Holt said, "and so are you."

Macie scoffed. "I'm far from a natural."

"It's true," he said. "I mean, you've relaxed in the saddle, and I think you're ready to ride on your own. Pull back on the reins."

She did, and before she could protest, Holt had dis-mounted. "Just keep her walking, I'll stay by you. Don't worry, Bonney's a good girl, and we don't have far to go."

"All right." Macie took a deep breath and flicked the reins. Riding the horse by herself was surreal. Soon, she was grinning.

Holt smiled up at her.

At that moment, Macie knew she wanted this, wanted *him*. There was no doubt in her mind. She couldn't have found a better man in Holt, and it seemed that he was equally interested in her. She could only hope that Knox wouldn't come and destroy it all.

"Mommy's riding a horse!" Ruby called out.

"I sure am, sweetie," she said. Then to Holt, "Now what do I do?"

"You rein Bonney to a stop, then climb down."

Macie did so, and even though Holt was close enough to help her, she managed to dismount without any trouble. She wanted to hug Holt and thank him for taking her riding, but Rex was only feet away.

"What did you think?" Rex asked.

"A little scary, but I loved it," Macie said, a happy buzz still coursing through her.

"Good to hear," Rex said, looking from Macie to Holt with the slightest crease in his brow.

What had that been for? There was no way Rex could know they'd kissed, right?

"I'll put Bonney away," Holt said.

Macie tried to focus on Ruby and her chatter after Holt disappeared inside the barn, but her mind was with him and what had happened between them on the ride. Then panic would flash through her at the thought of Knox showing up at the ranch soon.

"Mommy!" Ruby said. "Can I? Please? Please?"

"Please what?" Macie said with a laugh, sure that Rex had noticed her inattentiveness.

"Go with Grandpa to his meeting."

Surely, Rex hadn't invited a three-year-old to a meeting.

"How about after your nap, we go into town and get ice cream," Macie said.

Ruby looked both disappointed and happy at the same time. "Okay."

It was a minor miracle that Ruby hadn't thrown a fit. The three of them walked back to the barn. Holt wasn't inside the barn any longer, and Macie felt disappointed. She already missed him. Was he in the office? Could she come back after getting Ruby down for her nap?

When she got back to the house with Ruby and settled her for a nap after three stories, Macie went into the kitchen. She'd told Heidi to write out lists in the morning of what help she needed with dinner preparations. Now, she read the pink sticky note on the fridge. *Thaw chicken breasts in cold water. Slice tomatoes and cucumbers. I'm at a ladies' luncheon this afternoon.*

Easy enough. Macie was glad the woman was getting out for a little while. Heavy footsteps caught her attention as she was filling a bowl with water. Her first thought was that Holt had walked in, but then Rex came into the kitchen. For some reason, this flustered her.

"Hi," she said lamely. "Can I make you a sandwich or anything?"

"My meeting will include a lunch," Rex said as he crossed to the fridge. He pulled out a pitcher of juice, then poured himself a glass.

As he drank, Macie stayed busy with the chicken. Then she set to work on slicing tomatoes.

"What are those for?" Rex asked.

"Heidi put it on her list for me," Macie said. "Probably a salad for dinner."

Rex nodded and crossed to the kitchen sink, where he rinsed his glass out. "You've been mighty helpful to her."

"Oh, I'm happy to help however I can." Macie lifted her gaze for a second. "I'm grateful for all you've done for me and Ruby."

Rex folded his arms. "We're glad you came. Families shouldn't be separated for so long."

"I agree," Macie said, although her throat was feeling tight for some reason.

"But I need to tell you one thing, Macie, then I should get to my meeting."

At this, she set down the knife and turned her full attention on the man who had once been her father-in-law.

"You need to be mindful," he said. "Of everyone's hearts in the family." He straightened from where he'd been leaning against the counter, then snatched his cowboy hat from the table where he'd left it and strode out of the kitchen.

It was some time before Macie's hands stopped trembling and she could resume slicing vegetables. She paused yet again when another set of footsteps came into the house. These were lighter, but still a man's.

And when Holt slid his arms about her waist from behind, relief shuddered through her. Whatever his dad's opinion was, Holt's was what mattered.

"Hey, darlin'," Holt murmured. "Everyone gone?"

"Mostly," she said, placing her hands over Holt's and leaning against him. This was new, yet felt so comfortable at the same time. "Ruby's asleep, and I don't know how long your mom will be gone."

"Hmm," his voice rumbled. "So it's just us?"

Her belly fluttered. "Yes." She felt his smile against her neck just before he pressed a kiss there.

Then he kissed her below her earlobe. The scruff of his jaw sent her skin tingling. She turned slowly in his arms and gazed into his smiling blue eyes. Her heart soared, and she smiled back. "You're kind of a hands-on guy, aren't you, Holt Prosper?"

His hands skimmed over her arms, and then his callused hands cradled her face. "With you, always."

He kissed her as if it hadn't only been an hour since their last one. Macie had no problem returning his kisses, and she tugged his hat off, which made him chuckle. He backed her against the counter, trapping her, which only meant she was fully pressed against his lean body. She slid her hands along his neck and into his hair, pulling him even closer.

Holt's hands skimmed down her back, then tugged her hips against him.

Before she knew it, he'd lifted her onto the counter, dragging her legs around him. Holt was all man, and all hers. Everything about him was warm, delicious, intoxicating, and when her fingers trailed his torso, he drew in a breath.

"Macie, we gotta stop," he said, his breathing ragged as he moved his mouth to her collarbone.

"I don't want to."

"Me, neither, darlin', but I'm not going to be able to backpedal if we don't cool it off right now."

Macie paused, her heart rate crazy. "Okay. You're right."

Holt rested his forehead against hers as she slowly traced his shoulders. "I came in here to tell you something, but then I got distracted."

Macie smiled, but when she met his gaze, his blue eyes were serious. "What is it?"

"I'm going to start staying at my place in town," he said.

"The renovations have made it pretty unlivable, but I'll just sleep there, and eat here."

Macie felt like she'd been doused with cold water. "Why?"

His thumb skimmed her jaw. "I think you know. I won't be doing much sleeping with you only a couple of bedrooms away. And it's only going to be harder to hide my feelings about you from my parents when we're constantly in each other's proximity."

Macie exhaled. These were words that should be making her happy on one level, but her stomach had hollowed out. "And what are those feelings?" she whispered.

"That I can't stay away from you, darlin'," he said. "That I can't stop thinking about you. That I don't want to be apart for even one minute. I know it sounds crazy."

She pulled him into a fierce hug. "I know it's crazy, too, but I feel the same way."

15

HOLT'S NEW ROUTINE WAS working all right for the most part for the past three days. He'd show up just before dawn, get his usual coffee in the kitchen, then head out to work on the ranch. Macie was always in the kitchen, waiting, and sometimes, she made him bacon. And he even once downed a couple of pancakes.

Today, they were going riding, and Holt would be taking Ruby on his horse—to make things more platonic, and because it would keep any suspicions at a minimum. Holt was having a hard time keeping his thoughts and emotions to himself, and if his mom wasn't so wrapped up in her healing process, he was sure she would have noticed the change in him.

Holt felt like a new man. A man with a purpose. A man with hope and a vision of the future. One with Macie and Ruby in it. What that meant for Knox, he didn't know, but he'd cross that bridge later.

For now, Holt was thinking about how he'd spend a mellow afternoon with Macie and Ruby—who'd definitely become part of his life now. While he waited for them to arrive, Holt worked on the accounting in the barn office. Things were still pretty dismal, but he had several boarding commissions starting in a couple of days with cowboys arriving for the rodeo.

He'd charged them fifty percent down, and that had helped. Most of the ranch bills were currently caught up, with only a few things pending. This would be great if he could count on boarding animals throughout the year, but once summer was over, that would drop off drastically.

Last winter, he'd traveled quite a bit to help with consulting other horse owners. He might have to do that again this winter.

"I don't see him," came a young, petulant voice from the barn area.

"Maybe he's in the office," Macie said.

Holt smiled at the sound of her voice. Then just before he could lean back in his chair and open the door wider, Ruby burst through.

"I found him!" she said, then launched herself into his arms.

"Easy, little darlin'," he said with a chuckle, pulling her into a hug. "Nearly knocked this old man off his chair."

Macie appeared in the doorway, her brown eyes warm with amusement.

"Hi," he said over Ruby's head.

Macie tilted her head, a soft smile on her face. "Hi," she said back.

Holt did a slow perusal of her clothing. Plaid shirt, fitted jeans, cowboy boots, braided hair. It was as if she'd lived on a ranch her whole life. When his gaze met Macie's again, she grinned. "Approve?"

"Always."

"Ruby, baby, can you go count the horses?"

"Yes, Mommy!" She scrambled past Macie and hurried into the main barn.

Holt rose from his chair. "What was that for?"

"That was so you can come over here and kiss me," Macie said. "After looking at me like that, you'd better make good on it."

Holt chuckled, then he tugged her farther into the office. He pulled her close and lowered his mouth to hers. Kissing Macie was becoming like home to him. The happiest place he could be. She twined her arms about his neck and pressed against him.

Despite moments like these, immersed in their own bit of heaven, Holt couldn't help but feel like they were standing in front of a huge countdown clock. One in which his brother would emerge and shake things up. Macie had told Holt more than once that she had no intention of ever giving Knox a second chance, yet small doubts still edged their way into Holt's psyche.

He could only hope that they were able to build enough of a foundation with their relationship that it would be him who Macie would choose, not his brother. Again.

"Mommy! I counted! There's five horses!"

Macie released him and stepped back a half-second before Ruby careened into the office.

"Nice job," Macie said with a laugh, squeezing Ruby next to her. "Should we go ride one?"

An hour later, Holt sat near the stream while Ruby and Macie waded in the shallow water. They'd eaten the sandwiches that Macie had brought along, and then they'd explored and picked flowers.

Holt wished this day could go on forever. That every day could be like this.

"Hold my hand, Ruby," Macie said, as Ruby nearly tripped.

Holt loved watching the two of them together. He loved how Ruby copied everything her mom did, and how so many things were new to her. Ruby's wide-eyed view of the world brought a different perspective for him, too, one in which he could see his future working out how he'd always wanted.

"I caught it," Ruby said, then held up a flower she'd dropped in the water. "It needs to dry."

"All right," Macie said. They came out of the water, and Ruby released her mom's hand and ran to him. "Can you blow it dry?"

Holt reached for the wet flower. "I can try." Then he blew on the flower.

Ruby giggled.

He blew again, and Macie laughed.

She held out her hand. "I think we should put it on a rock and let it dry in the sun. You're going to get a headache with all that blowing."

"Very true," Holt said with a chuckle, then handed the flower back to Ruby. "Do you want to find a rock, Ruby?"

"Okay." She carried the flower like it was a piece of glass. She stopped at a larger boulder, then carefully placed the flower upon it.

"Perfect," Macie said. "It should be dry before we have to leave."

Ruby turned with a smile, then skipped back over to where Holt was sitting. She climbed into his lap.

Holt sent Macie a surprised glance, but she only smiled.

"Tell me a story," Ruby said.

"One story," Macie said. "I don't want you falling asleep, baby."

Ruby yawned as if on cue, and Holt laughed.

Macie settled next to him and said, "I want to hear your story, too."

"I don't think I know any stories."

Ruby looked up at him. "Please!"

"All right," he said, then launched into a story about a kid who grew up on a ranch and begged his grandma for a puppy.

Ruby nestled against his chest. "Someday, I want a puppy, too."

Holt met Macie's gaze and winced. "I'm sorry," he mouthed.

Macie moved her hand up his back, out of sight from Ruby, and Holt decided that the day couldn't get any better.

By the time they returned the horses to the barn, Ruby was good and tired. Holt carried her into the house, the little girl's head lolling against his shoulder. As Macie followed him into the bedroom where he'd laid her down, he said, "There's no reason you can't each have your own room with me staying at my place now."

Macie watched him settle Ruby on the bed, and she covered her with a blanket.

"Stay in here, Mommy," Ruby murmured, her eyes half-closed.

"Remember what I told you about falling asleep like a big girl?"

"I need to do it by myself."

"Right." Macie bent and kissed Ruby, then straightened.

"See you soon, little darlin'," Holt said.

He walked with Macie out of the bedroom, and she closed the door quietly behind them. Holt didn't know where his parents were exactly, but his mom could be napping in her bedroom, so he knew now wasn't a good time to kiss Macie.

Reluctantly, he put some distance between them in the

hallway. "I should head back to the office and get a few things done."

"There's that crease again," Macie said, reaching up to touch him between the brows.

"What crease?"

Macie trailed her finger along his skin, moving closer, which only sent his heart thumping. "You get this little crease when you're worried, and I've seen it more and more. What's bothering you, Holt Prosper? Is it me?"

Holt captured her hand and kissed her palm. "It's not you, and I don't want you to worry your pretty head about it."

Macie moved closer, so that they were only inches apart. "That's not how it works, Mr. Ranch Manager. I've confessed all my problems to you." She rested her hands on his shoulders. "If you can't tell me, then who can you tell? Your parents?"

"Definitely not my parents."

Macie held his gaze. "Holt . . ."

"All right," he said. "Come into the kitchen in case someone pops into the house. I don't want them to catch us kissing in the hallway."

Her smile appeared. "Is that what will happen?"

"You know it will." He bent to give her a quick kiss to prove his point, then pulled away and headed into the kitchen.

She laughed softly and followed.

Once in the kitchen, Holt knew he'd been right about coming here. He also knew he could trust Macie with the information about the ranch's finances. Maybe her entrepreneur's mind would give him some new ideas.

So with her sitting at the table and him leaning against the counter, he explained how the ranch had gotten into hot water.

"Your parents are sure generous folks," Macie said at the

end of his long explanation. "Makes me feel guilty for infringing upon their hospitality."

"You'd never be infringing, and I hope you know that,
darlin'."

Macie nodded, and he had to be satisfied with that.

"So what are you going to do?" she asked.

"Well, having Knox more independent would sure help,"
Holt said. "I mean, if he ever paid back his loans. And my
younger siblings becoming more independent would be great.
It's just life right now, I guess."

Macie rose to her feet and crossed to him. Linking their
hands together, she said, "If anyone can figure it out, it's you."

"How did you come up with that?"

Macie raised up on her toes and kissed him. He obliged
in the stolen moment, but the sound of an arriving truck drew
them apart.

Macie skedaddled across the room and picked up one her
jewelry kits from the side counter, then settled at the table
again.

Holt filled up a glass of ice water. "Want some?"

She shook her head and opened up her kit, so by the time
Rex Prosper walked into the kitchen, she'd already laid things
out.

His dad's gaze went from Macie, then to Holt, then
narrowed.

Holt had the sense that his dad had noticed a shift with
Macie, but he was still determined to not give away his true
feelings for her. Not until they figured out what was going to
happen when Knox arrived.

"You're both here," Rex said, uncertainty in his voice.
"That's probably better."

"Better for what?" Holt drained the last of his water.

"Sit down, son, we've got something to discuss."

By the time Holt sat across the table from his father, a knot had formed in his stomach.

His father took off his cowboy hat and turned it in his hands, his gaze dropped.

Holt met Macie's gaze across the table, but he had no answers, either.

"A short time ago, I received the list of rodeo entrants," Rex said.

Ah. Holt's stomach went hollow, and he rubbed a hand down his face.

Rex lifted his gaze. "You knew about this, didn't you?" he said to Holt. "For how long?"

"About a week now," Holt said. "Knox called me. Said he wanted it to be a surprise."

Rex exhaled, then tossed his hat on the table. "It sure was a surprise seeing his name on that list."

Macie hadn't said a word, and Holt didn't blame her. The air in the kitchen was thick with tension, but for different reasons for each person.

"What else did he say?" Rex asked.

Holt wasn't going to divulge what his brother had said about winning Macie back, so he said, "Says he wants to make amends." He left it at that, without going into greater detail.

After a moment, Rex stood from the chair, picked up his hat, and strode out of the kitchen.

Holt closed his eyes for a second. Knox's return wasn't going to be easy on anyone. When he felt Macie's hands on his shoulders after she crossed behind him, he placed his hands over hers and squeezed. He could only wish, only hope, that Knox's appearance wouldn't change what Holt had been building with Macie.

16

MACIE PARKED HEIDI'S CAR in front of the low building with a list of medical doctors on the sign in front.

"Here we are," Heidi said in a light tone.

Macie hadn't missed the undercurrent of stress in the woman, and she exhaled silently, then opened her door. "It looks like a nice place."

"Oh, it is," Heidi said. "They have new carpeting and indoor plants and everything."

Macie popped open her door, and then walked with Heidi into the waiting room. As Heidi signed in, Macie looked around. Several people were waiting, and a TV hummed in the corner, although no one was paying attention to it.

This waiting room could be any waiting room in the country. And these patients could all be in various stages of illnesses. Macie blinked back the stinging in her eyes, determined to be a support for Heidi, and not to feel sorry for herself.

By the time they left the appointment for the blood draw, Macie was more than ready to leave. The memories of such visits with her mom had left her feeling raw. But she'd managed to tamp all that down, and just focus on Heidi.

"Do you want to grab lunch at the café down the street?" Heidi asked as they climbed back into the car.

"Sure," Macie said, although she hated to leave Ruby for very long. She'd fallen asleep for her nap, and Rex had said he'd keep an eye on her when she woke up. But Macie knew that Heidi needed this outing.

Macie tensed as they drove farther into town. It was obvious that preparations for the rodeo were well under way. The place was busier than ever, and there was actually traffic. "Where should we park?" Macie asked when it looked like all the street parking was filled.

"Behind the café," Heidi said.

The woman didn't seem bothered by the crowds. Maybe she liked the busy aspect, but Macie wasn't entirely looking forward to more introductions. The ones at Racoons had been enough.

But the moment they walked into the café, Macie realized she'd been worried about the wrong thing. There sat Barb at a table with her girlfriends—the same ones from the other week. As usual, Barb was dolled up, looking like she was about to do a professional commercial.

"Oh, my goodness," Barb said, loudly enough for the entire café to hear. "If it isn't the Prosper women out in spades." She rose and strolled over to them, wearing a yellow halter top paired with white skinny jeans and yellow heels.

Soon, Macie was enveloped in a perfumed hug, then they were drawn over to the table.

"Make room, everyone; we've gotta catch up."

Jana and Patsy scooted their chairs over, and Barb managed to snag two more chairs in the crowded café. Heidi excused herself to use the restroom, and Macie was immediately pounced upon.

"Oh my goodness," Barb said. "Those men at Racoons were sure all over you. Have you been dating any of them?"

Jana and Patsy watched her like excited toddlers about to have ice cream.

"No, I'm not dating anyone," Macie said, keeping her voice as low as possible. It was true. She wouldn't really consider she and Holt dating, not in the formal sense, anyway.

"Well, Briggs has been asking about you," Barb continued. "Don't you think he's good-looking?"

Macie shrugged. She didn't want to comment too much, because all of these people in this town went way back in their relationships.

Jana giggled. "What does that mean? Yes or no?"

"It means that I'm not talking about dating." Macie smiled, hoping to lighten her tone.

"It's just us, hon," Barb rested her hand on Macie's arm. "You can't stay sad and single forever."

Macie's neck felt hot, and she wondered what was taking Heidi so long.

"So, tomorrow night, there's going to be a cattle parade," Barb continued. "Lots of smokin' hot cowboys will be there. How about coming with us?"

Macie's stomach dropped. Would Knox be there? The rodeo was still five days away. How soon would he arrive?

"I don't know," she said, primarily because the invitation caught her off guard, and brought up a well of emotions she didn't want to think about in a public café.

"Well, we plan to wear you down, hon," Barb said with a grin. "Right, girls?"

Finally, Heidi rejoined the group, and the chitchat moved to things that didn't have Macie wanting to hurry back to the ranch. Still, Macie had never been so glad to have lunch over when Heidi announced that it was time to head home. A flurry of hugs and kisses took place before Macie finally escaped out the back door.

Heidi's phone rang as she was getting into the car, but before Macie could sit down in the driver's seat, Barb rushed out of the back door.

Her blue eyes wide, she hurried to Macie, and after casting a glance at Heidi on the phone, she whispered, "Don't think I don't know what's going on between you and Holt."

Macie froze. "W-what do you mean?"

"I went over to his house yesterday, and he told me that he couldn't invite me in." Barb's eyes narrowed. "Said it wouldn't be *proper.*"

Relief cut through Macie. Barb was making a supposition, and she had no real information. But Macie couldn't hide the heat she felt creeping up her neck. "I don't know why you're telling me all this."

Barb's eyes flashed. "Holt likes *you.* I saw the way he looked at you the other night, and I can hear it in his voice when he talks about you." Barb latched onto Macie's arm, her long nails digging a bit too hard into it.

Thankfully, Heidi was still on the phone inside the car. "Barb—"

"Now you listen good, Macie," Barb said. "The Prospers are like family to me. If someone's going to mess with them, then I'm going to take it personally. Do you hear? Stay away from those brothers. You've done enough damage."

Macie couldn't have been more surprised if Barb had thrown water in her face.

Barb suddenly released her, spun on her yellow heels, then marched back into the café.

Macie didn't move for a moment. Couldn't.

Then slowly, she climbed back into the car with Heidi. The woman was still on her phone, chatting with someone who sounded like a neighbor. Macie started the car and pulled out of the small parking lot. Was what Barb said true? Was it obvious that Holt was interested in Macie? Did anyone else suspect?

She felt like her rosy bubble with Holt had just been popped. If Barb was reacting like this, how would Heidi and Rex feel? The rest of their family?

When Heidi hung up, she released a heavy sigh.

Macie glanced over at her. "Are you all right?"

"I'm just tired, dear," Heidi said. "It's exhausting pretending that I have energy."

Macie understood more than Heidi might know. She reached over and patted her hand.

"Thank you for coming with me," Heidi continued. "I know it's been a burden on Rex to always be worrying."

"The doctor seemed positive, right? Everything's on track."

"Right." Heidi lifted her chin. "That's what I keep telling myself."

Silence fell between them, and Macie sensed Heidi's melancholy, which made her wish she could do something about it.

They pulled up to the ranch, and Macie felt disappointed that Holt's truck was gone. Seeing him after the talking-to she'd received from Barb would have been nice. He'd have an answer in his assured and steady manner.

Macie found Rex and Ruby sitting on the big recliner, Ruby snuggled against her grandpa. The TV was on low.

"Did she just wake up?" Macie asked.

"No," Rex said. "She woke up soon after you left and said she didn't feel well."

"I'm sick, Mommy," Ruby said in her little voice.

Macie crouched before her and placed her hand on her forehead. Sure enough, Ruby felt too hot. "I'm sorry." She looked at Rex. "You should have called me." She felt guilty about being gone the extra time for the lunch. Missing Barb's comments would have been no sacrifice.

"It's all right," Rex said, smoothing back Ruby's hair. "I've been around sick kids before."

Heidi approached and felt Ruby's forehead, too. "Goodness, she's burning up."

Macie straightened. "Maybe I should take her to a hotel for a couple of days. I don't want her spreading germs." She very well knew that cancer patients shouldn't be around extra germs.

"Nonsense," Heidi said. "Everything's sold out with the rodeo, anyway. I'll wash my hands and keep separated as much as possible."

"Is grandma sick, too?" Ruby asked in her innocent voice.

"A little bit, sweetie," Macie said. "Here, let's go find some fever medicine. Then I'll lay down with you." She hoisted Ruby into her arms and carried her into the bedroom.

After getting her settled with a drink and a teaspoon of fever medicine, Macie lay down next to her daughter until Ruby's breaths grew even. Taking such a late nap would probably mess with her sleeping schedule that night, but that didn't matter right now.

Sometime later, Macie opened her eyes. Her first realization was that she'd fallen asleep right alongside Ruby, and her second realization was that the sound of a truck had awakened her. Her pulse immediately jumped. Holt must be back.

She listened for more sounds. The front door opened, followed by a murmur of voices—Rex's and Holt's. Rex said something about going to the barn, and then footsteps came down the hallway. Holt's. Macie's heart rate beat in tandem.

When the door cracked open, Macie turned her head. Holt stood there, hesitating. She motioned for him to come inside as she sat up.

Holt approached silently, his gaze going from hers to the sleeping Ruby.

"How's my little darlin'?" he whispered.

Macie moved off the bed and straightened her clothing. "Sleeping, finally. The medicine seems to be helping."

Holt's blue gaze scanned her face. "You're all right? You're not sick, too?"

"I'm fine," she said. "Your mom and I went to her appointment, then to lunch. Came home to find your dad had been doing double duty."

"I'm glad you're fine." He linked their fingers, and Macie's heart rate zoomed. "You look tired, though."

"I took a little nap," she said. "It's good to see you."

Holt's mouth curved, and Macie inched closer.

"Where's your dad?"

"In the barn."

Macie was pretty sure Heidi was taking her own nap, so she moved even closer to Holt. He smiled just before she raised up on her toes and kissed him.

"You *did* miss me, darlin'," he murmured against her mouth.

She only pulled him closer, and he chuckled, tightening his hold on her.

"I need to talk to you," Macie said. "Somewhere else."

Holt nodded, even though he was clearly curious. Macie led him to the kitchen after closing the bedroom door to let Ruby continue sleeping.

She filled a couple of glasses with peach lemonade from

the fridge and handed one to Holt. He leaned against the counter, took a sip of the lemonade, then said, "What's going on?"

Macie set her glass down. "We saw Barb in town, and while your mom was in the car on her phone, Barb confronted me."

Holt's brows pulled together. "About what?"

Macie relayed the entire conversation, then she said, "I don't know how much longer we can keep things a secret. And now that Ruby's sick, I should take her somewhere for a few days. I don't want her getting your mom sick, and every minute of the day, I'm waiting for Knox to show up and make claims he has no right to."

Holt set down his glass and moved closer to Macie. He laid his hands on both of her arms. "Don't you worry about Knox. I'll handle him. And don't you even think twice about leaving here. Maybe we should just tell my parents today. It will be a lot to lay on them, but I agree with Barb."

Macie stared at him. "You do?"

"If Barb guessed the truth," he said, "others will, too. And I'm no good at hiding my feelings for you." He gently squeezed her arms. "My feelings are getting stronger every day, darlin', and maybe they've always been this strong, but I've never allowed myself to hope until recently."

"Holt . . ." Macie whispered. She wanted to tell him she felt the same. But she wanted to get over the hurdle of Knox's appearance first. Have their relationship out in the open with Rex and Heidi. Know that she wasn't inflicting more pain upon the already injured family.

She moved her hands up his chest and ran her fingers over his open collar. Then she pressed a kiss at the base of his neck.

Holt's hands settled at her waist, and Macie wrapped her

arms about his torso and leaned into him. Holt pulled her into a tight hug, and for a few moments, they stayed like that. Macie closed her eyes, breathing in this man, his strength, his steadiness, and his deep core of loyalty. The sound of an approaching vehicle drew them both apart.

"I thought you said your dad was in the barn," Macie said.

Holt's blue eyes shifted from her to the kitchen windows. "Maybe it's Briggs." He released her and crossed to the window. "Damn."

"Who is it?" Macie said, joining him at the window. Then every part of her body went ice cold.

She'd know that black truck anywhere. She remembered the argument they'd had over the cost of getting it lifted.

Knox was back.

17

SEEING HIS BROTHER IN person was different than talking to him on the phone, and the first thing that Holt noticed was that Knox was clean shaven and wearing a dress shirt. His hat was also new, and his boots looked like he'd just pulled them out of a box.

There hadn't been any communication between them since that last phone call where they'd both threatened each other. And Holt knew that if he didn't head off his brother from busting into the house, things were going to escalate pretty fast.

"Stay here," Holt told Macie as he headed out of the kitchen.

"Holt, what are you going to do?" she asked.

He paused and turned. "What I should have done a long time ago."

Macie opened her mouth to say something, but Holt didn't have even a second to spare. He strode to the front door and swung it open.

But he was too late. His dad had come out of the barn and was walking toward Knox.

As soon as Knox saw their dad, he took off his hat and ran a hand nervously through his hair.

Holt paused on the porch as his dad continued toward Knox. He decided it was a good thing that Dad had a heads-up, but now Holt worried about his mom. Should they have prepared her?

But all Holt could think about was how this brother of his had treated Macie. Had used her, had cheated on her, had broken her heart. It was probably good that Holt remain on the porch while his dad did the talking for now.

"Hey, Dad," Knox said, setting his hands on his hips. "I thought I'd come by, you know, before all the rodeo stuff gets under way."

Rex nodded. "Saw your name on the lineup. Come to see your mother?"

"Yes," Knox said in a firm voice. "I need to apologize to you, too. Said some things that I shouldn't have."

Holt folded his arms.

Rex shifted his stance. "That so?"

"Look, I've done some growing up," Knox said. "You were right. About all of it. I should have . . . should have listened more and argued less." He kicked at the gravel beneath his boot. "I've been a damn fool, and I've lost my wife because of it."

Holt exhaled. Was Knox really going to confess?

Knox looked over at him. "Hey, bro."

"You made it."

Knox lifted his chin. "Yeah, I'm hoping to redeem myself a little. If not to the town of Prosper, hopefully to my family." His gaze went past Holt to the house. "Macie here?"

"She's inside." Holt held Knox's gaze, refusing to waver.

"Ruby, too?"

Holt nodded.

"I'd sure like to see them," Knox said.

Holt didn't like this version of Knox. Yeah, he'd wanted his brother to feel remorse and to step things up. But how would Macie react to this newer, humbler version of her ex-husband?

"I'll let her know, and she can decide if she's coming out," Holt said.

"I'm here," Macie spoke behind him, pushing through the screen door.

Holt tensed. Every fiber of his being went on alert. He wanted to look at Macie, see her expression when she looked at Knox. What was she thinking? Feeling? But he couldn't look at her right now, because he was having a hard enough time keeping his own emotions in check.

Knox took a step toward the porch. "Macie, sugar, I was hoping you'd be here."

Macie hovered on the porch, not going to greet him, which Holt considered a good thing.

Knox looked from Macie to Holt, then back to Macie. "I guess you heard I was coming into town for the rodeo."

"I did." Macie's words were clipped.

"Thought I'd spend time with Ruby, too, if that's all right."

Macie hesitated, then said, "Of course, it's all right."

Holt wanted to stand between the two. Prevent Macie from getting hurt all over again, and prevent Knox from wheedling his way back into Macie's life. But of course, that would be impossible. Ruby was involved, too.

"How have you been doing, sugar?" Knox said in a low voice, moving another step toward the porch.

Holt hated the tenderness in Knox's voice.

"I'm fine," Macie said. "Look, Knox, maybe we can talk later, but Ruby's been sick, and—"

"She's sick? What's wrong?"

"Just a fever—"

"Oh my goodness!" Heidi came out onto the porch, carrying Ruby. "Knox, you're . . . here. Oh my goodness." Her voice cracked, and Knox moved up to the porch steps.

"Hi, Mom."

Tears streaked Heidi's cheeks, and Macie moved to take Ruby from her arms. Ruby's hair was tangled, the color high on her cheeks, and she looked like she'd just woken up.

Knox hugged his mom, and she cried onto his shoulder.

Holt leaned against the railing of the porch and looked away. His dad was taking in the entire scene, and instead of a frown, he looked like he was moved at the reunion between mother and son.

After Knox released their mother, she said, "Ruby has been asking for you."

Holt's breath stalled as Knox turned to Macie, who was holding Ruby.

Ruby still looked wan, but her eyes were tracking every movement of Knox.

"You're my daddy?"

Knox's smile dropped, but he quickly recovered. "Of course, little darlin'."

Ruby lifted her head more. "Holt calls me little darlin', and he calls Mama darlin'."

The stiffness of Knox's shoulders told Holt that this was not well-received news. "That so?" He moved closer to Ruby and acted like he was about to take her from Macie.

But Macie said, "She's not feeling well, Knox, and she doesn't really know you."

At this, Heidi frowned, sensing the growing tension between the two of them. She placed her hand on Knox's arm.

160

"It's such a surprise that you're here. I didn't know you were coming. Why didn't you tell us?"

"It was sort of last minute," Knox said, his attention temporarily diverted. "Decided to enter the rodeo, and, uh, see my family."

Heidi rubbed his arm, her smile broad. "Just like the old days?"

"Sure, Mom," Knox said. "I can't tell you how much I missed your cooking."

Heidi chuckled. "Oh, your wif—er, Macie does most of the cooking now. She's been *so* helpful."

Knox glanced at Macie, appreciation in his eyes, appreciation that Holt didn't like in the least. "Thanks, sugar. I'm mighty obliged to you."

Macie's eyes widened as Knox addressed her. "It's not a problem. You have a wonderful family, Knox." Her words were pointed, and the flush on Knox's neck told Holt that this was a discussion they'd had before.

"I get to ride a horse!" Ruby announced. "Grandpa and Holt teached me how to take care of it."

"That so?" Knox's gaze slid to Holt's. "Sounds like you've become a regular cowgirl."

Ruby giggled. Her energy seemed to be slowly returning. "Holt says I have to wear boots to ride Sammy, and they're pink!"

Again, Knox was looking at Holt.

Holt stayed leaning against the railing, keeping his arms folded, not saying a word.

"Mommy, put me down," Ruby said. "I want to show Daddy my boots."

Macie looked like she was about to say no, then she set Ruby down. The little girl hurried into the house. Knox watched her go, then cleared his throat. "Look, uh, I'm glad you're all here. I needed to apologize to everyone, especially Macie. I let some things get the better of me, and I was . . ." His gaze cut to Holt's, then returned to Macie's. "I was unfaithful, and no woman deserves how I treated Macie."

Heidi gasped and covered her mouth, tears starting again for a different reason now.

Knox pressed on. "I wanted y'all to know that I'm real sorry, and I'm a new man. I'm here to own up to my mistakes, and be the husband and father I should have been from the beginning."

No one else moved. No one spoke. Then Ruby's pattering footsteps sounded from inside the house, coming toward the door.

"Look, Daddy!" Ruby called before pushing open the screen door.

Knox crouched before Ruby to inspect her pink cowgirl boots. "Those are real pretty, doll."

Macie turned from the scene and walked down the porch steps, then continued walking toward the barn. No one stopped her. Knox continued to talk to Ruby, asking her questions and laughing at her responses.

It was clear he was nervous and hadn't interacted with a lot of little kids. Holt wondered how long this whole charade would last.

"Where's Mommy going?" Ruby asked.

That's when Knox noticed that Macie had left. He straightened and told Ruby, "Can you stay with Grandma for a bit? I need to talk to your mom."

Ruby nodded, clearly eager to please this new adult in her life. Knox crossed the porch to the stairs, but Holt grasped his arm. "Hold up."

Knox turned with surprise, then his brows drew together when Holt didn't release him. "Let her be."

Knox jerked his arm away.

"Let's go get a treat in the kitchen, Ruby," Heidi said, and ushered the little girl into the house.

Which was probably a good thing, because Holt wasn't in a charitable mood.

"Leave me be." Knox headed down the stairs and strode past Rex.

Holt took off after him. "She's not your wife anymore, Knox. You have no right to interrupt her peace here."

Knox whirled at this. "You don't get to tell me how to run my life, or how to talk to Macie."

"Son," Rex said in a commanding tone. "Holt's right. You showing up and expecting everyone to forget the past in a couple of minutes isn't realistic. These things take time. If you're truly serious about changing your life, then you know you'll always be welcome. But Macie needs time and space. You two can work out how you're going to raise Ruby, but that's a discussion for when Macie's ready."

Knox's throat worked as he swallowed.

Holt could tell that he was holding back plenty of retorts.

"Don't tell me you're taking Holt's side on this?" Knox ground out.

Rex didn't blink. "What are you talking about? *Macie* did the right thing in my opinion, cutting you loose so that you can finally decide what kind of a man you want to be."

Knox's face flushed. "What am *I* talking about? It's as clear as the blue Texan sky that Holt is carrying on with Macie. He's still sore at me for taking her to the dirt dance that night we all met. Hell, they're probably sleeping together by now—"

Holt reached Knox in two steps and drove his fist into his brother's jaw. Knox was a strong guy, but caught by surprise, he staggered and fell to the ground.

A gasp from the front porch told Holt that his mother had seen, and the little girl crying told him that she had Ruby with her.

Knox scrambled to his feet and rammed into Holt.

"You piece of sh—" Knox shouted, but Holt cut him off with a punch to the gut.

Both of them went down. Fists flying.

Someone screamed, and Holt could swear it was Macie. Had she turned around? He was too preoccupied trying to prevent his brother from breaking his nose to pay much attention. It seemed the drinking and womanizing had caught up to his little brother after all, because soon, Holt had Knox pinned in the dirt.

"That's enough," Rex said in a steely tone.

Chest heaving, Holt got to his feet. Seconds later, Knox scrambled up and away from him.

Knox's lip was bleeding, but he wasn't much worse for the wear. Pointing a trembling finger at Holt, he said, "You're not going to get away with this. You think you can take everything from me? Well, you've got another thing coming."

He snatched his cowboy hat from the ground, then strode to his truck. Engine roaring and tires spinning in the gravel, Knox took off without looking back.

18

MACIE'S HANDS TREMBLED AS she set clothing into her suitcase. Ruby was curled up on the bed, having cried herself to sleep. She was still sick, poor thing, and Macie felt bad she was having to take such drastic action right now. But the best thing to do was find another place to stay until she figured everything out. Yeah, she and Knox would have to work out things with Ruby if he insisted on living near wherever she was. But that didn't need to involve the entire Prosper family.

Not Rex, who'd looked disappointed; not Heidi, who looked betrayed and shocked; and not Holt, who looked like he was going to track down his brother and continue their fight.

Someone tapped on the bedroom door.

Macie wiped at the tears on her cheeks, then went to answer it. Holt stood there, one hand braced against the door frame. Her heart hitched just looking at him. They'd been living in a fantasy world the past few weeks, and it had all come crashing down today.

His parents had found out about them in the worst possible way, and the brothers had gotten into a physical fight over her. This couldn't be her life. She couldn't allow this angst to continue.

Nothing but complications and trouble had risen out of her relationship with Knox. Macie wished she could just take Ruby and start over someplace new. Even as she thought it, she knew she couldn't deprive Ruby of her grandparents.

"Hey," Holt said in a soft voice. "My parents want to talk."

Macie looked away. "I already said I'm sorry, and I think it's best that I leave for now." She started to shut the door, but Holt put his hand out to stop it from closing.

"Macie," he said. "My mother was surprised, that's all. She had no idea. Whereas my dad already suspected."

Macie blinked. "He did?"

Holt released the door and reached for her hand. "Please, darlin'. None of us want you to leave."

Tears flooded her eyes. "That's sweet, but I can't stay."

"Okay." Holt brushed his thumb over her fingers. "But at least come talk to them. There's been a lot of confusion, and we need to all get on the same page. Especially for Ruby's sake."

His searching blue gaze told Macie that it wasn't just for Ruby's sake. It was for whatever might be left of her relationship with him. This was something Macie couldn't let her mind go to yet. Because she was pretty sure things between them had ended the moment Holt had punched Knox.

"All right," she whispered. "Give me a minute, then I'll come out."

Holt squeezed her hand, then let go and stepped back. She shut the door with a quiet click. Turning, she leaned against the door and closed her eyes. She breathed in, then out. At the very least, she owed an explanation to her former in-laws. Heidi had been thinking a good marriage counselor would be the answer to Macie and Knox's reconciliation, and now . . .

Macie wiped at her cheeks and smoothed back her hair, then she left the room. She heard a low murmur of voices coming from the kitchen. When she entered, everyone stopped talking. Holt stood and pulled out a chair for her. Then he sat on the opposite side of the table. Macie took the chair, glancing between Rex and Holt, and then finally looking at Heidi. Which proved a hard thing to do.

The woman's crestfallen expression and red-rimmed eyes only made Macie feel worse.

"Thanks for coming, darlin'," Holt said. Just like that, he'd called her *darlin'* in front of his parents, as if he had no qualms about it.

Macie wasn't sure what to think.

Surprisingly, Rex spoke next. "I'm really sorry you've been caught between my two sons this way, Macie." He steepled his fingers and sighed. "I had hoped that Knox had been a better husband to you, and that your divorce was because of irreconcilable differences. You might not think I should be doing the apologizing for my son, but I'm apologizing anyway. Holt filled us in a little more than what came out of Knox's glossed-over confession, and I'm ashamed that a son of mine would do such things."

Heidi covered her mouth and closed her eyes. Rex reached across the table and grasped her hand. "I know Heidi feels the same way, but a mother's love runs very deep."

Macie blinked at the new tears forming. "Of course, I understand. I'm sorry as well for not letting you know the true nature of my marriage. I didn't want to hurt anyone more than they'd already been hurt. I thought that it could stay in the past, and I could move forward from it. But my past mistakes have a way of sticking, I guess."

"No one is blaming you for anything," Holt said.

Her gaze connected with his. His blue eyes held hers—his gaze steady, resolute, warm. She looked down at her clasped hands as tears dripped onto them. "I can't be here," she whispered. "I feel like I've torn your entire family apart."

Rex shook his head. "Knox did that all himself. We've given him multiple chances to change, and although I had some hope today, it's clear that his motivations are still not pure."

"He came here to apologize," Heidi said in a strained voice, pulling her hand away from her husband's.

"And look what a mess he made of it," Rex shot back. "Accusing Holt and Macie of—"

"Dad," Holt cut in. "Knox knows of my feelings for Macie. He knew of them before he came back."

Macie stared at Holt.

"And it's true that I have always harbored something for Macie," he continued. "Knox acted out of impulse and anger, which might have been justified when he was still married to her. But now, he has no leg to stand on. He gave up the best thing to happen to him."

Heidi took a shaky breath. "What about you, Macie?" she asked in a trembling voice, "Did you come to the ranch because of Holt?"

"Mom—" Holt interjected.

Macie lifted her hand. "It's okay. Your mom deserves an answer. Your dad, too." She rubbed the sides of her neck with both hands, exhaling. "My only intention of coming to the ranch was for Ruby to get to know her grandparents. I didn't expect to feel things for Holt." She blew out a breath. That wasn't entirely true, so she tried again. "When I met Holt all those years ago, I found him attractive. I was nineteen years old, and my friends dared me to go meet a cute cowboy."

Macie winced at her own words. They sounded so trite and immature. "So I started talking to Holt. I liked him, yeah, in the way that any girl might like talking to a handsome cowboy. But when Knox asked me to the dirt dance, it wasn't hard to shift my focus. I didn't know either of them, not really. The entire night was a new experience for me. First rodeo, and first . . . of a lot of things." She didn't need to go into more detail. They were all adults here, and her message was clear without further embarrassing anyone.

"But I will say, Mr. Prosper," she continued, looking at Rex, "you've raised a fine son in Holt. I never thought the man of my dreams could exist." Her voice shook. "It turns out he does. But there's a huge hurdle because he's Knox's brother. I hope you believe me when I say that I was blindsided by how my feelings could shift."

No one said anything. Would they believe her? "I know that it's best that I leave the ranch. I can't keep hurting your family." She met Rex's gaze. "Can you give Ruby and I a ride to the next town where I can find a place to stay for a couple days while I make decisions?"

"You can stay at my house," Holt said. "I'll move back here."

Heidi pushed back from the table and went to stand by the kitchen sink. She folded her arms and gazed out the window. Macie couldn't guess what was going through the woman's head. And she couldn't look at Holt right now.

"I can't chance running into Knox right now," she said, "so I need to leave Prosper altogether."

"Is that what you really want?" Rex asked, his tone even, not betraying what he thought of her confession.

"Yes," Macie whispered. In a stronger voice, she said, "If you'll excuse me, I need to finish packing. Then we'll be ready to head out."

Rex gave a small nod. Heidi said nothing.

And Macie wasn't going to stick around to hear Holt's response. She rose from the table and hurried to her temporary bedroom.

She needed to stop crying. She had to be strong. What had she expected to happen when Knox came into town? Surely, she knew he'd find out about her and Holt at some point. Knox was competitive, and Holt was loyal to the core. No matter the scenario, the outcome was going to be devastating.

She could do this . . . start over. She'd done it before. More than once. Her mother's death hadn't broken her. Her unplanned pregnancy, her shotgun wedding, her divorce . . . Macie was strong. She was a mother now, and focusing on Ruby should be her top priority anyway.

Once she was packed, the tears had long dried, although her heart had gone completely numb. She opened the bedroom door and rolled the first suitcase down the hall.

Rex was in the living room, sitting in his chair, not reading or watching TV. Holt was still at the kitchen table. Heidi was nowhere to be seen—probably back in her bedroom.

When her gaze connected with Holt's, she had to look away immediately. In that instant, she'd seen the questions and regret all rolled into one. She didn't want to start crying again.

"Let me help," Holt said, rising to his feet.

"I got this one," she said. "You can grab the second one." Ruby's car seat was already in Rex's truck from when he'd taken her for ice cream the day before. Macie headed toward the front door, not able to handle much more conversation.

Once she reached the truck, she unlatched the tailgate, then hefted the suitcase onto the truck bed.

Soon, Rex arrived, carrying the second suitcase.

Following him, Holt walked out onto the porch, a sleeping Ruby in his arms.

Macie almost started crying again at the sight of Holt carrying her daughter. Ruby was going to miss him. And her grandparents. Macie knew she'd be enduring days of endless questions.

Without a word, Holt set Ruby in her car seat. Her head lolled to one side, and Holt placed one of her stuffed animals next to her head for a cushion. Macie had forgotten to pack it—Ruby must have been sleeping with it.

Rex climbed into the driver's side and started the engine.

Macie reached for the passenger door, but Holt put his hand on hers before she could pull it open.

"Call me when you get to wherever you're staying."

"Holt—"

"Please."

She could hear his breathing, feel the warmth of his strong hand atop hers. "Okay," she said at last, then lifted her gaze to meet his.

His blue eyes searched hers for answers, ones that she didn't have.

He leaned down and kissed her cheek, then released her hand and stepped away from the truck.

Macie didn't want this. Didn't want to say goodbye to him. She wanted to throw her arms around him, bury her face against his neck, and have him hold her until the pain stopped.

Instead, she opened the door and climbed into Rex's truck.

19

"WELCOME TO THE FORTY-ninth annual Prosper Rodeo, folks!" Rex Prosper's voice boomed across the arena. "Let's give it up for our loyal organizers and committee!"

The arena erupted in applause as Holt leaned against the edge of the fence by the bullpens.

Rex continued with introductions and recognizing sponsors while Holt scanned the area behind the bullpens for his brother. Tonight was the last night of the rodeo, and the first night that Holt had come. Knox was in the top five bull-riders and was heading into the championship round. He'd clocked out over eight seconds both of the previous nights.

Holt hadn't spoken to his brother since the incident at the ranch. He'd finally texted him yesterday, but no reply from Knox.

Being at the ranch was painful. His mother stayed in her room most of the time, and his father had gone silent. So that left Holt feeling plenty guilty. Not about Macie. Never Macie. He'd never change any of his decisions the past few weeks with her. No . . . his guilt was that his mother didn't have the relationship she'd always wanted with Knox. And that things could have been restored between Knox and their dad if Holt hadn't responded so drastically.

The other side of his mind continued to argue. Sometimes, a man needed to be set in his place. And sometimes, a woman needed defending.

A clown, who was the true master of ceremonies, made his way to the middle of the dirt arena. He began telling jokes and had the crowd laughing in no time. The bull-riding would be one of the final events, so there'd be plenty of time to find Knox beforehand. But there was no sign of him.

Holt straightened from the railing and headed out of the arena, then walked toward the parking lot filled with horse trailers. Everyone was busy, preparing for their events. It was another ten minutes before Holt found Knox sitting on a camp chair next to a young woman. Holt's gut tightened as he observed what was obviously flirting. The woman wore a white sequined shirt with turquoise jeans. With her dolled-up makeup, he guessed she was in one of the rodeo events.

"You got anything to give me for good luck?" Knox was saying as Holt approached from behind the pair.

The woman laughed. "How about one of my earrings?"

"Don't you need it?" he asked.

"No one will notice," she said with another laugh, then undid her earring and handed it over.

Knox held it in his palm. "It's right pretty, and if I win the championship, I'll buy you a brand new pair."

"Knox," Holt said.

Knox's fingers closed over the earring, and he turned.

"Been looking for you," Holt said, completely ignoring Knox's scowl and the woman's curious expression.

"That so?" Knox said, returning his gaze to the woman. "I'm busy at the moment."

Holt moved so that he was facing the couple. "This will only take a second."

Knox's jaw worked, and Holt knew he was battling to protect whatever image he'd created with this newest woman.

"Sugar, can you give me a second with my brother?" Knox said at last.

"Oh, he's your *brother*?" The woman's interested eyes landed on Holt again.

Well. All the guilt that Holt had felt over punching Knox had completely fled now.

The woman rose from the chair and strutted away, but not before giving a flirtatious wink to Knox.

He tapped the brim of his hat in acknowledgment.

"This better be quick," Knox said.

Oh, it would be quick. Holt sat in the camp chair the woman had vacated. "I have three things to say. First, Mom is wrecked, and if anything, you owe her a visit. Second, Dad knows nothing about your debts, and as of now, they are all forgiven. You don't owe me another cent, but you'll also never get another loan. Third, if you harass Macie in any form, I'll be sure to help her file a restraining order."

Knox's green eyes had gone black. "We share a kid."

"That can be changed in court."

Knox's jaw clenched. "You can't be serious. Macie's just trying to get back at me. There's no way she wants anything serious with you."

"She moved out right after you left," Holt said. "I don't think she knows what she wants, but if she wants me, then nothing's going to stand in our way."

"Is that a threat?" Knox ground out.

"It's a promise."

Knox scoffed.

"I don't know if you ever loved Macie," Holt said, "at least in the way she deserved. But obviously, you're not trying to get her back. You haven't changed, and I don't see that happening anytime soon. So I'm here to tell you that if Macie and I have a future together, just know that if you want to have a relationship with Ruby, you'll need to clean up your life."

"You have no power to tell me what to do," Knox shot back.

"You're right. Only you have power over yourself." Holt rose from the chair. "But you have a little girl out there who doesn't even know her daddy. Maybe one day, you'll want to change that. And as much as I want to throw another punch at your face right now, for Ruby's sake, I hope you'll man up one day and be a decent father to her."

Knox shot to his feet, eye to eye with Holt. "You have no right—"

"Goodbye, Knox." Holt stepped back. "Call Mom. Get your life together. And honestly, I hope you win the championship tonight. I hope you use the money to get out of debt and make good on something in your life."

Holt turned and walked away. He didn't think Knox had an answer anyway. Holt had come to say what he needed to. Knox was a grown man, and Holt couldn't babysit him anymore.

"Holt Prosper, is that you, pumpkin?" Barb's voice rang clear.

He looked over to see her standing with a couple of women. Her yellow rodeo outfit glittered in the lights, blending with her blonde hair and white cowboy hat. Holt didn't even break his stride.

"Barb," he said, tipping his hat.

Continuing past, he pretended he didn't hear her next question. It was time to get out of here. Time to get in his truck and drive out of town. And hopefully, Macie would answer her door.

It wasn't until Holt had driven past the city limits that his pulse began to slow. The rodeo would be over tonight, and hopefully, Knox would be gone tomorrow. Holt wanted to convince Macie to return to the ranch when Knox left.

He drummed his fingers on the steering wheel, thinking of all the upheavals in Macie's life over the past few years. He hated to think that she was suffering yet again. But she'd only given him short replies to his texts, and he'd felt effectively cut off.

The past few days without being around Macie had left a hole in his heart, one that he knew only she could fill. He also missed Ruby.

When Holt pulled up to the motel where Macie was staying, he grabbed a sack of things his mother had sent with him. She wasn't willing to call Macie yet, but she wanted Ruby to have some treats.

The motel was more rundown than Holt was comfortable with. He also didn't like that she didn't have a car. He walked the perimeter until he found her room number. He pulled out his phone and texted her that he'd arrived. When he'd texted her earlier that night to tell her he wanted to stop by, there'd been no reply.

Still nothing.

Holt knocked softly on the door. He waited a moment, then finally, he heard something from inside, then the door opened.

Macie stood there, a thin bathrobe pulled about her. Her hair was tied up in a knot, with damp tendrils curling against her neck. Plainly, she'd been in the shower or bath recently.

"Holt." His name came out on an exhale.

"Did you get my texts?" he asked, even though he knew they'd been read.

Macie lifted a hand to her neck. "I did, and I wish you wouldn't have come all this way. Ruby's asleep, and I'm not good company."

Holt braced a hand against the door frame. "I wanted to make sure you're okay."

Macie held his gaze for a moment, then looked away. "I'm okay. I already told you that."

"I wanted to see for myself." He looked down the length of the motel. "This isn't the best location to be staying by yourself." His gaze shifted back to her. "I can pay for a nicer location. I want you safe."

She lifted her chin. "It's fine, and I'm fine, Holt. I was being serious when I said that I don't want any handouts."

"It's not a handout, darlin'," he said. "Not when you're family."

But she didn't soften, and she didn't relent. He could see the determination in her eyes—determination to stick her ground.

He examined the door. There was a doorknob lock and a rather flimsy chain link. He took a step into the hotel room and rattled the loose contraption. "This should have a dead-bolt," he said. "At the very least. Do the windows lock?"

Macie folded her arms. "They're locked."

He glanced over at the small sleeping form of Ruby in the single queen bed. He hated that Macie and her daughter were so exposed and vulnerable here. He moved past Macie and walked to the window. He parted the drapes, then tested the lock.

"I guess you're coming in," Macie deadpanned.

He looked over at her. The door was still open a foot, and she stood by it, her lips pressed tight.

"Please let me help you relocate," Holt said.

"Ruby's asleep for the night," Macie said. "Besides, you can't keep worrying about me."

Holt closed the distance between them. "I'm going to worry about you when you're two towns over and staying in a dump with who knows what on the other side of the door."

Macie exhaled and looked down. "That's not what I mean."

Holt didn't miss the sorrow in her voice. "Do you want me to leave, then?"

For a moment, he thought she'd say yes, but instead, she stepped toward him and slipped her arms about his waist. He shut the door with one hand, then pulled her close.

She smelled like warm apples, and he simply breathed her in, relieved that she'd hold him, and that she hadn't kicked him out. Yet.

"You don't give up, do you?" she whispered against his neck.

Her breath on his skin sent goose bumps scattering across it, and he closed his eyes. "Not when it comes to you, darlin'. I've missed you."

Her hold tightened on him. "I just want him to go away."

Without asking her to clarify, Holt knew she was talking about Knox.

"But that wouldn't be good for Ruby in the long run," Macie said, drawing back and meeting Holt's gaze. "Why does it have to be so complicated?"

"You're a loyal person, Macie," he said. "And you've got a big heart."

"He says that he wants to be able to talk to Ruby when he's not in Texas."

"Knox called you?" Was it good news that Knox had

179

requested visits? This was a step forward, right? More than he'd done over the past year.

"Yeah," Macie said in a quiet voice. "A few minutes ago."

"What else did he say?"

Macie met his gaze, her green eyes resolute. "He told me that if I wanted to . . . pursue you . . . then he wouldn't put up a fuss."

Holt stared at her, because he wasn't sure where she was going with this, but his hammering heart was hoping it would be positive.

She bit the edge of her lip, which only made Holt's attention go to her mouth. "So . . ." he said

"So . . ." she breathed. "I told him that I didn't know how things would turn out between you and me. But that I appreciated his support."

Holt raised a hand and ran his thumb along her jaw. "Am I allowed to hope? Or are you going to break my heart?"

Macie's eyes fluttered shut as he moved his hand behind her neck.

"Your mom hates me."

"No, she doesn't," Holt said. "She'll come around." He moved one hand slowly down her back. "She's just had a shock."

Macie's eyes opened. "What about your dad?"

"You heard him the other day," Holt said. "He doesn't want to see you suffer anymore, and he'd do anything to help."

Macie nodded, then bit her lip. "Can we take this one day at a time, Holt?" she whispered.

"I can live with that," he murmured, just before his mouth claimed hers.

She twined her arms about his neck and tugged him closer. Holt obliged, although he didn't let his hands wander.

Ruby might be asleep, but they weren't alone. Besides, he wanted Macie to be sure about him. No doubts whatsoever.

But the fact that she was kissing him back and didn't seem like she was about to let him go anytime soon was more than good enough for Holt.

20

IT TURNED OUT THAT a week away from Holt was much too long. The night he'd visited her, he'd kept guard in his truck outside her motel room. She'd finally agreed to relocate to a different hotel the next morning with his help.

He was one stubborn man. In the best way possible way and in every way opposite of his brother.

"What's that?" Ruby asked, sidling up to Macie where she sat at the hotel desk, browsing a website on her laptop.

Macie pulled her daughter onto her lap and drew her close. In all of this, in all that had happened, Ruby had made every heartache worth it. This child born of her had brought Macie comfort when nothing else could.

"That's an apartment in San Antonio," Macie said.

"A swimming pool?" Ruby touched the laptop screen.

"Yep, do you like it?"

"I wanna swim, Mommy."

"Of course you do," Macie said with a smile. She rested her chin atop Ruby's head and continued to click through photos of the apartment complex. There was a playground, a community barbeque area, and a swimming pool, and the one-bedroom apartments were in her price range.

She'd decided to stay in Texas. Ruby deserved the best, and being near her grandparents would fulfill that requirement. But San Antonio would also give them some distance that Macie needed from the Prosper family to sort out where she fit.

"Should I call them?" she asked.

"Yes!" Ruby said.

Macie laughed.

"Can I watch TV?" Ruby asked.

"All right, just for a little bit," Macie said. She hated that Ruby had been watching so much TV in the hotel room, but really, their options were limited right now. Anything to distract her from incessant questions about when she could ride Sammy again or get ice cream with Grandpa or make pancakes with Holt or read stories with Grandma.

Macie wanted all of these things for Ruby, but it wasn't like she could waltz back onto the ranch as if nothing had happened between the two brothers.

She called the apartment complex and found out that tours were open anytime between 9 a.m. and 6 p.m. After hanging up, she pulled up the bus schedule app she'd downloaded to her phone.

Before she could decide on a schedule, her phone buzzed with a text from Knox.

I need your help.

Macie frowned. What could he be referring to? Her pulse thumping, she wrote: *What is it?*

Her phone rang, and with Ruby wrapped up in her TV show, Macie answered it.

"Are you still in Prosper?" Knox asked.

He knew she'd left, so the question confused her.

"No, I'm in a hotel."

Knox paused. "Can you get to Prosper by tonight? It's Mom's birthday, and I'm not going to make it."

Of course he wasn't. "Where are you now?"

"I'm hitting a few other rodeos in Texas, and I'm going to try to qualify for the pro-circuit. You know, the PRCA."

Macie held back her sigh. Knox had failed at qualifications the past three years for one reason or another, but maybe winning the Prosper Rodeo had upped his confidence again. He'd sent her five hundred dollars, out of the ten thousand in winnings.

"Okay, so you want me to take her flowers or something?" Macie said. "Those can be ordered, Knox." She could only imagine the awkwardness of showing up to see Heidi, a woman who thought she'd betrayed and used both of her sons, and telling her happy birthday.

"Flowers or whatever is fine," Knox said. "But I know what she really wants is to see her grandkid. It's all she talks about when I call her."

The good news was that Knox was calling his mother again. The bad news was him bringing Ruby into the conversation. It only compounded Macie's guilt for keeping Ruby away from the ranch. Macie closed her eyes against the twisting in her stomach. There would probably be others at the ranch if they were doing any sort of birthday celebration.

Macie did not want to be around a bunch of Prosper residents—the questions would kill her.

Ruby giggled at something on the TV. She really was being such a good girl. So patient with her emotional mother.

"Was that Ruby?" Knox asked.

"Yeah."

"Can I talk to her?"

This was another first. "Of course."

Macie unfolded herself from the chair and walked over to Ruby, who was perched on the edge of the bed. "Sweetie, your daddy wants to talk to you."

"Oh!" Ruby snatched the phone. "Daddy?"

Macie couldn't help but smile at Ruby's enthralled expression as Knox's voice rumbled through the phone, asking her questions.

"Okay, Daddy, I promise!" She handed the phone back to Macie.

What had Ruby promised?

"Are you still there?" Knox asked.

"It's me," Macie said.

"Ruby said she'd tell her grandma 'happy birthday' for me."

Macie should be annoyed, even mad, because Knox was definitely manipulating the situation. But she shoved her first reaction to the back of her mind. "Okay, we'll figure it out." By that, Macie didn't know if that meant going to Prosper or maybe calling Heidi.

"Thanks, sugar, I appreciate it more than you know," Knox said.

"Don't call me sugar."

Knox chuckled. "Macie—"

"I mean it," she said, moving away from Ruby. "You can sweet talk other women all you want, but I don't want to hear it."

He didn't say anything for a moment, then finally, "Fair enough. But thank you. Truly."

Macie exhaled slowly. Civility. She could do this. "You're welcome."

Moments later, when she'd hung up with Knox, she still had no idea how the future would work between the two of them. Would it be littered with random phone calls to Ruby? Maybe a visit once in a great while?

She sat down at her laptop, and then her phone rang again.

Holt.

What were the chances? Every conversation with Holt over the past week had been him trying to talk her into coming back to Prosper, and her telling him that she wasn't ready yet. Holt saying he understood, but if she changed her mind . . . Her telling him that she'd let him know.

"Hello?" she said into the phone.

"Hi, darlin'."

This was one man she wouldn't tell to lay off the endearments. Even if she wasn't sure of the definition of their relationship right now, his endearment was like a cozy blanket. "Hi."

"What have you been up to today?" His deep voice rumbled through the phone, sure and calm like usual.

"Well, Ruby slept in, so I got all my orders finished early," she said. Mundane stuff, but Holt always asked and was always interested. "We'll head to the post office soon, then we're going to San Antonio to check out an apartment complex."

"So you decided on San Antonio, huh?"

"Possibly," Macie said. "It's a pretty place."

"Yeah . . ." He let the word linger, and she knew he wasn't saying what he wanted to. "I can drive you."

The offer was sweet, and leading. She could only imagine how it would be spending the day with Holt, wrapping himself tighter and tighter around her heart. "Thanks, but I already figured out the busses. It will be an adventure for Ruby, too."

Holt chuckled. "That it will be. But if you change your mind, darlin'—"

"I know, I know, I have your number," Macie finished, unable to stop the smile from emerging.

"When you get back, I was thinking I could pick up you and Ruby," Holt said. "Maybe get some dinner, and if you're so inclined, we could join my mother for a small birthday celebration."

Macie went quiet.

"My siblings are all coming in, and a few other miscellaneous Prosper relatives," Holt continued. "They all want to meet Ruby. And of course, I'd love for them to get to know you, too."

His words only veiled what he'd told her more than once. He wanted her in *his* life. He wanted the Prosper family to get used to Macie being with *him*.

"I don't know," she said at last. "I'm still figuring things out."

"Maybe coming tonight will help you figure out some of those things."

He was probably right, but she'd still had no communication with Heidi, and Macie didn't want to belabor the point to Holt. He'd tell her he'd talk to his mom, but that wasn't the right approach, either. Heidi shouldn't feel pressured by Holt.

"Whatever happens," she said, "I hope your mom has a wonderful birthday."

"I'll keep my phone on, and I'll check it maybe a hundred times."

Macie laughed, but she felt a pang in her heart, too, because she knew that although Holt might be teasing, she'd heard the affection in his tone. How did she get so lucky to have a man like Holt being so sweet on her? "You're not going to get much work done if you do that, Mr. Ranch Manager."

He chuckled. "I'm good at multitasking, darlin'."

She missed him. She missed seeing his face. Hearing his laugh in person. Feeling his arms about her. Breathing him in.

After she hung up, Ruby asked, "Who was that, Mommy?"

"It was your Uncle Holt."

Ruby bounced off the bed. "Can I ride Sammy today?"

"Not yet," Macie said. "We're going to look at that apartment with the swimming pool, remember?"

"Hooray!" Ruby clapped. "Then can I ride Sammy?"

The requests would never end, Macie knew. "We'll see," she said at last.

"If I'm a good girl?"

Macie held back a laugh. "That will certainly help."

The bus ride to San Antonio was a wonder for Ruby, and Macie was pretty sure she'd never heard so many questions in her life. Everything from "why does a bus smell funny?" to "why is there gum on the floor?" were just the beginning.

As they toured the apartment complex, Macie decided she liked the place well enough. It would be a lot different than living at the ranch, of course, but it would be nice to have Ruby interacting with other kids on the playground or at the swimming pool.

"If you sign this week, we're offering $250 off the security deposit," the office assistant told them.

"Good to know," Macie said.

As they headed back to the bus stop hand in hand, Ruby skipped alongside her.

"What did you think?" Macie asked, although she was pretty sure she knew the answer.

"I love it!" Ruby declared. "Can Sammy move here, too?"

"I'm afraid not," Macie said, holding back a laugh. And . . . they were back on topic with horses.

When they arrived at the bus stop, they still had thirty

minutes to wait for the next one. Close by was a small antique store. Macie thought they might as well browse to pass the time.

"Ruby, can you promise not to touch anything if we go inside that store for a moment?" she asked.

Ruby scrunched her nose. "What store is it?"

"It sells things that are old and very valuable."

"Okay."

As they walked through the store, Macie was charmed with many of the items, although she knew there wasn't any way to afford them.

"Look, it's me!" Ruby said, pointing to a metal sculpture of a girl on a pony.

Macie paused in front of the sculpture, holding Ruby's hand tightly. "I love it." The dangling price tag put the thing close to $1,000.

"Can I help you?" someone said, and Macie turned to look at an older man with nearly white hair and a rather impressive mustache.

"We're just browsing," Macie said.

"It's my grandma's birthday today!" Ruby announced.

Macie flinched. Her daughter forgot nothing.

"Is that so?" the shopkeeper said. "Does she like antiques?"

Ruby shrugged. "She reads me books."

"Ah, so you're a reader," the shopkeeper said in an amused tone.

This reminded Macie . . . "Do you have any first editions of mystery novels?"

"I have a few things along that line from estate sales," he said. "Come this way."

Ten minutes later, Macie had purchased a signed copy of

a hardback mystery. Even if Heidi had read it, she probably didn't have a signed copy, right?

As the bus pulled away from San Antonio, Ruby sat next to her, the wrapped book clutched against her chest as if it were the greatest treasure on earth. Macie exhaled and closed her eyes. Maybe she could stop in for a short time tonight to wish Heidi a happy birthday. Having Ruby with her would be an ice breaker, and Macie wouldn't need to deal with Heidi one on one anyway.

She opened her eyes and pulled out her cell phone from her purse.

Then she called a number she'd never thought she'd utilize.

21

"THANKS FOR COMING, HOLT," his mother said, kissing him on the cheek.

"Happy birthday, Mom." He pulled her into a hug. Then he stepped aside, because his other siblings were waiting their turn.

His youngest brother, Lane, and sisters, Cara and Evie, had all arrived with him. He'd planned it that way since he wanted to talk to them for a few minutes alone before the party. Holt had explained the events surrounding Macie and her daughter. Everything. Well, mostly everything, but they knew enough.

Lane had only shaken his head. Cara had asked a bunch of questions about Macie and Ruby. Evie hadn't seemed to care one way or another.

His mom already had a house full of people. Several neighbors were there, and the ladies she sat on committees with fluttered around the kitchen overseeing the food.

"Hey, cousin," a woman said. "It's been a while."

He turned to see his cousin Kellie, grown up from the blonde teenager he remembered. She used to spend summers at the ranch back then, but Holt couldn't remember the last time he'd talked to her. "Wow, great to see you." He pulled her into a hug.

"You, too," Kellie said after drawing away, a broad smile on her face. She was a pretty woman, petite, but definitely with spunk in her blue eyes.

"I didn't know you were in Prosper again," he said.

"I'm not," she said. "At least not officially. I'm here to do an interview for the newspaper. I thought it would be fun to interview in person. And, you know, see my cousins."

They moved out of the way of more people entering the house and settled on the couch in the front room, while most people had congregated in the kitchen area. "An interview, wow. What's it for?" He felt bad that his mind was drawing a blank on any recent news about her life.

"Well, you know about my divorce a couple of years ago, right?"

Right . . . He nodded. "Yeah, tough, I'm sure."

Her gaze dropped, but then she shrugged and said, "It was really rough, but I also learned a lot about myself and relationships. Why they get sabotaged, and how to pick up the pieces after. I decided to put my licensed therapy work to a more personal use. So, I started running retreats from my parents' ranch house. Well, I guess it's my place now since I inherited it." Her laugh was light. "I named the retreat Broken Hearts Ranch."

"Sounds interesting, I think."

Kellie smiled. "Well, it's not for people like you. Unless you've had your heart broken and can't move on in life."

Holt swallowed. Kellie was hitting a bit too close to home.

Her smile faded. "Oh, no. I'm sorry."

"It's not that exactly . . . well, things are complicated."

Kellie nodded. "If you need someone to talk to, I'm a professional now. Putting my license to good use."

"I appreciate that, but I'm not sure even counseling can sort out the fact that I've fallen in love with my brother's ex-wife."

Kellie didn't speak for a moment, and Holt didn't blame her. The words had just shot out of his mouth, and were probably way too much information for anyone to hear about, but they'd been said. And it would be a lie if he took them back.

"You're serious, aren't you?" she said in a quiet voice.

"Dead."

Kellie placed her hand over his. "When did all of this happen? I thought I heard Knox was here, and Heidi said something about Ruby staying at the ranch part of the summer."

Holt gave her a brief rundown, including the fistfight.

Kellie's eyes widened. "Whoa. That's kind of intense."

For some reason, this made Holt laugh. "To say the least."

"So, now what?" Kellie asked. "I mean, Knox is gone again, and where are Macie and Ruby?"

"At a hotel the next town over."

Kellie smoothed back her blonde hair. "You know . . . I have an opening in my next retreat."

Holt shook his head. "I'm good."

She leaned a bit closer. "For Macie."

Just then, the door opened again. Not that Holt had been exactly paying attention to who was coming and going at the party, but his attention was snagged anyway.

Macie walked in with the last person he'd ever expect in a hundred years.

"Oh my gosh, this party is rockin'," Barb declared.

Macie stood on the other side of Barb, but it was obvious

they'd come together. Barb was decked out in a candy red blouse, red-and-white striped capris, and red nails longer than should be legal. Holt much preferred what Macie wore. A white blouse tucked into faded jeans that followed her curves. She was wearing the boots he'd given her, and that fact made a bubble of pride rise to his throat.

Ruby was clutching her mom's hand, but as soon as Ruby spotted Rex, she broke away. "Grandpa!"

There were enough people milling about that Macie hadn't yet seen Holt sitting on the other side of the room with Kellie.

Barb led her toward the kitchen, chattering up a storm.

Huh.

"That was Macie and Ruby?" Kellie asked, breaking into his thoughts.

"Yep." He met her gaze. "What are you grinning about?"

"You're a goner, cuz." Kellie shook her head, still smiling. "And if I'm guessing right, her showing up tonight is a big deal, and neither of you will need my ranch retreat."

"I hope you're right," he said. "No offense to you."

She laughed. "None taken. Now, introduce me to your sweetheart." She stood and motioned for him to join her.

"I'm going to need a few minutes," Holt said. "At least until Barb isn't latched onto her like an octopus."

"Barb? Do I hear a story in that?" Kellie teased.

"Nothing to tell, much to her dismay."

Kellie laughed. "All right. Catch you later, cuz."

Holt leaned back on the couch as Kellie moved off into the crowd, greeting and interacting with people. He was impressed with how she'd turned her challenges into a way to help others.

And now . . . Macie was here. He brushed off his questions as to why she hadn't called him for a ride. No matter. He could forget that little detail. She'd come, hadn't she? But was it only for Heidi, or had she wanted to maybe reestablish her place at Prosperity Ranch and with him?

More people arrived, and the house was getting packed. It seemed that half the town had come to wish Heidi Prosper a happy birthday.

Holt slipped out onto the front porch. The night air was refreshing, and he set off down the porch steps. A light inside the barn was on, and he needed to check it out.

"Hi there, Mrs. Johnson and Mrs. Miles," he said as two older women arrived.

Holt continued toward the barn, only to find Lane inside, leaning against one of the corrals and stroking a horse. Lane was a younger version of their mom. Blonde hair, blue eyes. He'd always been the quiet brother. More introspective, and a whiz in academics.

"Hey there," Holt said. "Needed an escape?"

Lane glanced over at him, then turned back to the horse. "She's pretty."

"Bonney's always been a fine horse."

"I meant Macie."

"You met her a few years ago at Christmas."

Lane nodded. "It was brief, and I probably wasn't paying attention to a pregnant woman hiding out in the bathroom."

"Yeah, she's had it rough."

Lane said nothing.

Holt waited, because he was pretty sure his brother had more of an opinion on the matter. He was right.

"I'm sure you've considered this from all angles," Lane began. "And looked at all the scenarios."

Holt scrubbed a hand through his hair. "Correct."

"And I assume there's no changing your mind or redirecting your intentions."

"Correct again."

Lane nodded.

It wasn't a simple nod, but an accepting nod. "Then I vote you tell her that."

Yeah . . . Lane was probably right. Holt released a breath. "It's complicated."

Lane met his gaze then. "If anyone can manage complicated, it's you, Holt."

Holt didn't know if this was a compliment he wanted.

"Also . . . I peeked into the office and saw the junk mail from debt consolidation companies. What's going on?"

Holt froze. Yeah, his little brother was a numbers whiz, but what did he know about financial debt?

"Come on, Holt," Lane said. "I'm no dummy. And I'm guessing that you haven't told Mom or Dad about any of this."

"You're right." Holt drummed his fingers atop the corral. "Things have been tight since Evie started college. With three of you . . . it was to be expected. But then Knox went through his divorce, and I lent him some money. Multiple times."

Lane's jaw clenched, but he said nothing.

"So, last winter, I made the rounds throughout Texas," Holt said. "Did some freelance training and rehabbing rescue horses. Got the coffers built up, but then I returned, and Jerry had let things slide. A lot. Turned out his knee had been bothering him, so instead of letting Dad know, he just did the bare bones."

"You talked him into getting surgery?" Lane asked.

"That's right," Holt said. "Spent all spring catching up. Knox kept the begging up, and finally, I started lending to him from my own savings. Jerry's still recovering. Macie and Ruby showed up. And the offers are rolling in from the debt consolidation companies." He gave a self-deprecating laugh. "A bit messy, I guess."

"Has Knox paid anything back?"

"No," Holt said. "But I've effectively cut him off. I don't expect to hear from him for a while after he won the championship last week."

Lane rubbed at the back of his neck. "Well, I've taken business finance and business marketing, and I think you have some options open to you. You know, there's grant money out there for rescue horses. You could turn a profit when you have them rehabilitated."

"Something to look into, I guess."

"And no more loans to Knox," Lane said. "He'll have to find a regular job like everyone else when his ten grand runs out. And you need to talk to Dad, at the very least. He needs to be made aware. The ranch belongs to all of us, and you shouldn't be the only one shouldering this burden."

"I wanted to wait until I had better news."

"I'll find some for you," Lane said, stepping away from Bonney. "Mind if I look at the accounting, and maybe go over it with one of my professors? See what he recommends?"

Holt didn't love the idea, but Lane had impressed him thus far. "All right. I'm definitely interested in new options."

"Also, this might be tougher to hear, but I think Jerry's gotta retire," Lane said. "You can't have the ball dropped when you're gone."

Holt went quiet.

"Think about it," Lane said. "You can hire some new buck who's eager to please."

"Wanna move back and do online school?" Holt asked.

Lane smiled. "As much as I love this place, I don't necessarily want to work the rest of my days playing in the dirt and chasing horses."

"Ha." Holt clapped a hand on his brother's shoulder. "Don't let Dad hear you say that."

"Now, let's go meet this lady of yours." Lane moved past Holt.

"So, you're okay with all of this?" Holt asked, following him.

"If there's a woman out there who can make my oldest brother all googly-eyed, then I'll support the relationship."

22

FROM THE CORNER OF her eye, Macie had seen Holt leave the house. She wasn't sure where he'd been when she arrived, but she'd seen his truck.

Was he upset with her? Surely, he knew she was there. Barb had made sure their entrance was noticed by everyone. And in Barb fashion, she'd demanded the truth about her and Holt when Macie had called and timidly asked for a ride. She didn't want to ask Holt because he'd only be too sweet and kind and she couldn't keep leading him on if his mother was truly set against them. Macie couldn't bring herself to cause the Prosper family any more pain.

So, Barb it had been. And once Macie told Barb, that yes, she and Holt had been seeing each other, Barb was all in. Maybe it was the gossip-monger in her, but she'd done a one-eighty.

All Macie could do right now was stick close to Ruby. It would keep Macie's mind and hands occupied. Because she had yet to greet Heidi. Ruby currently sat on Rex's lap, with her hovering nearby.

Other family members were here as well—ones Macie

had probably met if they'd been there that one Christmas she'd come with Knox.

A blonde woman approached. "Hey, I just wanted to introduce myself. Kellie Prosper."

"A cousin?" Macie asked in a bright tone that she didn't feel.

"That's right," Kellie said. "How are you liking Prosper?"

"It's great," Macie said. What else could she say, surrounded by all these people?

"Yeah, Holt caught me up."

Macie stared at the woman. There was a lot of meaning behind her words. "He did?"

Kellie placed her hand on Macie's arm. "If there's one thing I can say, it's that the Prosper family is strong. A little setback isn't going to last long, so maybe take your gift over to Heidi. See what happens."

"Oh," Macie said, her hand tightening on the gift bag she'd been gripping for the past twenty minutes. "Am I that obvious?"

"Only to me." Kellie winked. "I'm kind of observant, though."

Macie nodded, feeling the nerves twist her stomach hard. Heidi was at the kitchen table, smiling over something an older lady was telling her. She'd opened a couple of presents, telling people they shouldn't have brought anything, but still smiling about it.

"Ruby." Macie bent to eye level with her daughter. "Do you want to help me give Grandma her present?"

"Yeah!" Ruby slid off Rex's lap.

Macie gave him a grateful smile, and he winked. She decided that was the shot of courage she needed.

Macie perhaps gripped Ruby's hand a little harder than

necessary as they moved around a couple of people, then arrived at the table where Heidi was holding court.

With no reservation, Ruby wrapped her arms about Heidi. "I love you, Grandma."

Heidi smiled down at Ruby, then kissed her on top of her head.

It was so simple for children. Their love wasn't weighed down.

"Mommy bought you a present," Ruby continued.

At that, Heidi raised her gaze to Macie's. Her smile was more polite than anything.

"Yes," Macie said, trying to keep her tone unaffected. "We were in San Antonio earlier today, and we found something we thought you might like." She handed over the gift bag.

Heidi drew out the book wrapped in tissue paper. When she uncovered the book, her brows lifted in interest. "Signed by the author?"

"It's a first book!" Ruby said.

"A first edition," Macie clarified.

"I've read some of this author's later books, but not this one." She opened the front cover. "How lovely."

"And there's more," Ruby said, shoving the bag closer to Heidi.

As Heidi reached into the bag and withdrew a smaller gauze bag, Macie held her breath.

Heidi undid the ribbon tie, then pulled out the bracelet that Macie had made for her. She wondered if Heidi would remember . . .

"Oh, it's the serenity bracelet." Heidi turned it over a couple of times, then slipped it on. "It's lovely, dear."

In that short sentence, gratitude flooded through Macie. Heidi's words had been sincere, and Macie couldn't ask for more. When Heidi raised her gaze to meet Macie's, her eyes were moist.

Macie swallowed against the growing tightness in her throat. "You're welcome."

Heidi's smile was genuine this time. "Well, I think Holt would be mighty glad to see you back at the ranch. I can keep Ruby with me while you go find him."

Now, Macie's eyes were the ones to fill with tears. Had she heard Heidi right?

"A-all right," Macie said. "If you're sure?"

The question had multiple layers to it. She knew it, and Heidi knew it.

But Heidi's nod was resolute. "I'm sure."

So Macie moved through the crowd, returning greetings to those who spoke to her, but not really seeing them because of her blurred vision.

Holt had probably left. Regardless, she needed to be outside for a bit. To think. To comprehend. To wonder.

She made it onto the porch.

And stepped right into a Prosper sister discussion.

She recognized both of them, although it had been years since she'd seen Cara and Evie. They were young women now and not teenagers.

"Hi, Macie," Cara said.

Both women were blonde, although Cara was more of a dirty blonde.

"Hi, nice to see you both." She gave Cara a hug, and it wasn't as awkward as she thought it would be.

Then she hugged Evie.

"Ruby is adorable," Evie said.

"Oh, thank you," Macie said, her nerves fluttering like mad.

"Looking for Holt?" Cara asked.

Macie flushed. What did these sisters know, or not know? "Uh..."

Evie laughed. "He and Lane are in the barn. Lane's probably boring him with statistics or something. The drive to Prosper was so painful with him telling us about how we need to be better at budgeting."

Cara nudged her sister. "Just because our brother's a nerd doesn't mean you need to make fun of him. Someday, he'll be richer than your husband."

"I'm not even dating," Evie shot back.

"What happened to that football player?"

At this, Evie blushed. "That was last week."

Cara laughed. "And this week?"

"Someone else that I'm not telling you about."

Macie smiled. She'd never had this: bantering with a sister . . . college . . . dating guy after guy.

"Oh, look," Cara said. "Speaking of men. There are our brothers now."

Macie looked beyond the porch to see Holt and who had to be Lane coming out of the barn. Her heart hitched just seeing the tall form of Holt striding in the direction of the house.

In a few moments, they were at the porch, and Macie didn't want to meet Holt's gaze, because her emotions had surfaced again.

"Nice to see you again, Macie," Lane said, extending his hand.

She shook his hand. "Great to see you, too. How's school going?"

Cara rolled her eyes, and Evie groaned. "Don't get him started."

Lane cut them a glare. "What's up with you two?"

"Come on, Evie, let's get some food." Cara smiled at Macie. "See you later."

"Okay," Macie said, smiling back.

"Come on, Lane," Evie said, grabbing her brother's arm. "Give them privacy, will you?"

Macie's eyes widened. Had Evie just said . . . ?

The siblings disappeared into the house, and Macie was left alone with Holt. She turned slowly. His blue eyes were on hers, his expression both amused and curious. "Hi there," she said.

"Hi, darlin'."

His words made her skin feel like it was gradually burning. How was he always so effortlessly handsome? No cowboy hat tonight, and his hair looked like he'd ran his fingers through it plenty of times. The edge of his jaw showed a couple of day's stubble, and his open-collar shirt revealed the base of his tanned throat.

Macie slipped her hands into her back pockets. "I was coming to look for you."

One of his brows lifted, his eyes not missing a thing. "You were?"

"Yeah." Macie exhaled. "I was, um, going to see how you were doing."

His mouth curved. "I'm doing fine."

"Good," she said. "That's good to hear."

Holt nodded, still studying her. "Want to go for a walk?"

"Okay," she said immediately.

"After you," he said, motioning toward the stairs.

She moved past him, catching his familiar scent of soap and pine.

They walked around the barn and toward the arena. The moon was nearly full and cast everything into a pale yellow glow. Macie folded her arms, not that she was cold, but because she suddenly didn't know how to be or act around Holt. When they reached the empty arena, she propped her arms on the railing.

Holt stopped next to her. "Beautiful night," he commented.

So it was going to be small talk, she guessed. It was true, though. The night was beautiful—a velvety darkness with only a whisper of a breeze. The low hoot of an owl sounded far off. "It was nice to see Lane and your sisters again."

"Uh-huh." Holt leaned against the railing, facing the opposite way.

She glanced over at him, then away.

"I'm glad you decided to come," he said.

"Yeah, well . . . I knew it was the right thing, even if your mom didn't really want to see me."

"Like I said, she'll eventually come around."

"She already did," Macie said in a quiet tone.

"What?"

"Ruby and I gave her a present." Macie then explained the rest of what Heidi had said to her. "So . . . I think that means she's okay with everything. I mean, you and me, together."

Holt didn't move, didn't speak for a moment.

Now, Macie's pulse was racing for another reason. Once they crossed this line, things would be more official. What if after all of this, Holt had changed his mind? She stole another glance at him. He still hadn't moved, but his eyes were trained on hers.

"Say something, Holt," Macie said. "You're making me nervous."

He lifted one of her hands from the rail, then brought it to his mouth. He pressed his lips against the back of her hand in such a gentle gesture that it took her breath away.

Then his other hand wrapped around her waist as he drew her away from the fence. Macie's heart hammered as he slid both of his arms around her, then leaned his forehead against hers.

"Do you think you could be happy with me, darlin'?" he murmured.

Her breath hitched. "I'm already happy with you."

He smiled, but said, "I mean all of what comes with me. Here. The ranch. Living in Prosper. I know it's asking a lot, and that you have plans in San Antonio."

She closed her eyes as he trailed his fingers along her jaw. "How long will you wait for me?" she asked.

His fingers continued down her neck then across her collarbone, as if he were memorizing her. "As long as you need."

"So you'd wait six months?"

"Mmm hmm," he rumbled.

"A year?"

"Sure thing, darlin'."

She slid her hands up his chest, over the soft cotton of his shirt, then behind his neck. "Two years?"

"Yep."

She heard the smile in his voice.

"You're a patient man, Holt Prosper," she teased.

"Just tell me when, darlin'—tonight, tomorrow, or in five years—and when you're ready, I'm going to ask you to marry me."

The night had stilled, and not even the breeze made a sound. It was quite possible that her heart had also stopped. "You can't mean that," she whispered. "I've only been in Prosper for a month."

Holt lifted his head and released her to cradle both sides of her face with his hands. "Remember that one summer day when you brought me peach lemonade and told off ole Briggs?"

Macie smiled. "Yes."

"That was the moment I knew I'd fallen in love with you." He shifted one of his hands behind her neck. "It took me a little longer to accept my fate. But I love you, Macie, with all my heart."

She blinked back the hot tears that had sprung up. "How is this possible?"

"Maybe I can't explain it, but it happened," he said. "And there's no going back for me now."

"Me, neither." She ran her fingers over the stubble of his jaw. "I love you, too." The words were so simple, yet they opened the floodgate of tears. She drew in a shaky breath and blinked as her tears fell.

Holt used his thumb to soak up the tears on her cheeks. "Then marry me, my darlin'."

She covered her mouth to stop the sob that threatened to break through.

Holt leaned in and kissed her jaw, then he moved her hand and kissed the edge of her mouth. "Whenever you're ready. But promise me that you'll be mine." His lips brushed against hers.

Macie's eyes fluttered shut, and he kissed her again. Lingering this time. "I don't want to wait that long," she murmured.

"So, only a year then?" Holt whispered, then kissed each of her closed eyelids. The scruff of his chin rasped against her cheek.

"More like a few months," she whispered back. "I never got a wedding dress the first time around, so I need time to shop. I don't want a quick ceremony again. I want something real with you."

Holt's hands were back to cradling her face, and his mouth crashed down upon hers.

Macie curled her hands around his shirt, holding on as she lost herself in this man who was better than anyone she could have ever dreamed up.

Holt's kissing slowed, and his hands skimmed over her shoulders, then down her back to her waist as he anchored her against him. She threaded her fingers into his hair, relishing his warmth, his scent, his solidness. Goose bumps raced along her skin as Holt continued to explore her mouth, sending darts of fire throughout the rest of her body until she was pretty sure her feet were tingling. When Macie was forced to catch her breath, she released her hold on Holt bit by bit.

"Does this mean you're coming home now?" Holt whispered against her mouth.

"You don't want to commute to San Antonio to see me?"

"Hell, no."

Macie laughed. "And here I thought you were being the hero and being patient."

"Hmm." Holt kissed the edge of her jaw. "That was then, this is now."

She couldn't stop the grin spreading. He continued to trail kisses along her jaw, the stubble of his chin tickling her.

"What am I going to do with you, Holt Prosper?"

"You're going to marry me."

She laughed again. "Okay."

He lifted his head to gaze at her. "Is this official then, darlin'?"

She nodded, her eyes pricking with tears. "Yes." Her chest felt like it had expanded so much that it was hard to take a full breath.

Holt pulled her into a bear hug and buried his face against her neck. Macie clung to him, her heart soaring.

Macie wasn't sure how long they spent at the arena, but eventually, Holt reminded her that there was a household full of people who were probably wondering where they were.

"Should we return to civilization?" he asked, his voice rumbling against her ear.

"I guess."

Holt chuckled, then he linked their fingers, and they walked back to the house. A few of the vehicles had left, and a rendition of "Happy Birthday" was being sung inside the house. Holt squeezed her hand as they walked up the porch steps.

"Ready?" he asked, pausing before opening the front door. He was still holding her hand.

Macie looked down at their intertwined hands, then back up at him. Walking into the Prosper household, hand in hand, would be making a statement. Loud and clear. "Ready," she said.

Holt leaned down and brushed her mouth with his. Then he straightened and opened the door. Together, they walked inside, still holding hands.

23

IT HAD BEEN FIFTY-three days.

Not that Holt was counting. Okay, so he'd been counting. But today was his wedding day, and he was already late. Only something really important could have made him late for his own wedding, and it was the news that Prosperity Ranch had been awarded a grant for rehabilitating rescue horses.

He'd already forwarded the email to Lane, who'd been the one to do the laborious part of the grant application. Holt couldn't explain the relief that he'd felt at receiving the email. Money would funnel in on a regular basis, and he would be able to sell the rehabilitated horses to new owners. Now the ranch's finances could finally be put in order, and he wouldn't have to travel so much away from home. They could even bring on a part-time ranch hand.

Holt checked his appearance a final time in the bedroom mirror. He felt like a cardboard cutout figure in his tuxedo, but Macie had insisted on going all out. And he was pretty much pudding in her hands.

His phone started ringing again as he headed downstairs to the main level of his house. So far, his mom had called, his dad had called, Lane had called, and now this was the fourth call in a matter of twenty minutes. He answered with a clipped voice without even looking at the caller ID. "I'd be there already if I didn't have to keep answering the phone," Holt said, striding into his newly-renovated kitchen to look for his keys.

"Whoa, you're late to your own wedding?"

"Knox?"

"Hey, man."

Holt paused in the middle of the kitchen.

"I'm not going to make it after all," Knox said.

Holt hadn't thought otherwise, even when their mom had said that Knox was planning on coming. Heck, if the roles had been reversed, there was no way Holt would watch one of his brothers marry his ex-wife.

"No problem," Holt said. "We appreciate the good wishes."

"Thanks, man," Knox said. "I didn't expect to wake up this morning feeling like I'd been crushed by a boulder."

Holt sat at the barstool, ignoring the texts now buzzing his phone. He and Knox had started talking about two weeks ago. At first a text here, a text there, then a conversation every couple of days. Knox had yet to come back to Prosper since he'd finally earned a spot on a pro-rodeo circuit.

"I want you to know that I wish you and Macie all the best," Knox said, his voice sounding strained but sincere. "I really do. Macie is . . . she's one in a million."

This was also a one-eighty-degree turn for his brother, and Holt swallowed against the tightness of his throat. "Your support means a lot, Knox."

"Can you, uh—" Knox's voice failed for a moment. "Can you tell Ruby that I love her, and that I'm going to visit soon?"

"Sure thing, man." Holt cleared his throat. "I'll let her know. She'll be thrilled to see you."

Silence fell between the two brothers. And for a moment, Holt wished that Knox was here. In his kitchen. So that he could hug his brother.

"Well, you can't be late to your own wedding, bro," Knox said at last. "We'll catch up later."

"Yeah," Holt said. "Right. Let me know how tomorrow's rodeo goes."

"Will do."

The two of them hung up, and Holt rose from the barstool. He spotted his keys by the toaster, and he snatched them up, then strode out of his house. He had a wedding to get to.

The church was only a couple of blocks away, but Holt probably should have walked. Apparently, the residents of Prosper loved a wedding, and his mother had invited everyone. Holt parked his truck in front of a fire hydrant. He figured if there was a fire, he could rush out and move his truck, right?

He didn't even check his phone as he strode to the church, because it would only slow him down more. Organ music played inside, and Holt stopped dead in his tracks the moment he stepped over the threshold. He didn't know so many people could fit inside the chapel, or so many flowers. In fact, people were standing along the sides of the pews.

And hundreds of pairs of eyes had swung around to look at him.

Holt lifted a hand and gave a little wave. Was that appropriate?

He thought he heard someone snicker. Sure enough, he turned to see Lane, who was holding back a laugh.

"You'd better get up there," Lane said, looking like he was

five years older when wearing a tux. "I think we're on the tenth run-through of the music."

"Right now?"

Lane clapped a hand on Holt's shoulder. "Right now."

Holt eyed the crowd. Most had turned to face the front again, but plenty were still looking at him. "Isn't there a side entrance for the groom?"

"Wouldn't know," Lane said. "Might as well walk up the aisle. Everyone already knows you're late."

"Good point," Holt muttered. So he walked up the aisle, nodding to those who greeted him. He saw several cousins, aunts, and uncles mixed in, but his immediate family was nowhere in sight.

After nodding to the reverend, Holt took his place, then he noticed his mother in the front row. She was already dabbing at tears with a wad of tissue. Holt gave her a reassuring smile.

The music immediately shifted into the wedding march song. It was like the organist had been watching his progress and started the moment he took his place. The stately notes filled the chapel, and everyone turned to look toward the back, anticipation buzzing through them.

Holt's pulse skyrocketed.

His sister Cara appeared first, wearing a pale violet dress and holding onto the arm of Robert, one of their cousins. The two walked down the aisle, and Robert nodded to Holt as he took his place on the groom's side. Next, Kellie came down the aisle, wearing the same color dress but in a different style, escorted by another cousin, Nate.

Kellie and Macie had hit it off, even when Holt had told Macie that the only therapy she was getting would be from him and nothing at Kellie's Broken Hearts Ranch. Both women had laughed a long time at his expense.

Then Evie walked down the aisle, also in violet, escorted by Lane, who was Holt's best man. Holt supposed in a different time or place, Knox might have been his best man. But their complicated situation had prevented that.

And then Ruby came along, walking down the aisle wearing a frilly violet dress. Her hair was full of sparkles that Holt remembered her begging Macie for. He wanted to laugh at her persistence, but his heart was too full right now to do anything but gaze at the little girl.

She carried a small white basket tied with purple ribbons, and as she walked, she scooped out flower petals, then dropped them on the ground. Sometimes it was one petal. Sometimes it was an entire handful.

A few people in the audience chuckled, but mostly they smiled at her adorableness. Ruby arrived at the front, and Evie took her hand, but then Ruby squirmed away and moved over to Holt's side. She set her small hand in his, and if this went against protocol, he wasn't about to change a thing.

And then it was as if the entire congregation drew in a breath at the same time.

Macie appeared, escorted by his father.

Holt was pretty sure his heart had lodged itself in his throat. Macie's smile was nervous, but the second their gazes connected, it turned genuine.

Holt grinned back, knowing that he was completely giving himself away. He didn't care. Macie was the love of his life, and he wanted everyone to know it.

She looked stunning, and Holt wondered if he was still asleep, dreaming this.

"Mommy's pretty," Ruby said.

People close enough to overhear her tittered.

Holt squeezed her hand. "She sure is, little darlin'."

Macie wore a cream-colored dress with a V-neck and elegant lines falling to the floor. The fabric rippled with fluidity as she walked slowly down the aisle. Her dark hair was pulled up, off her neck, and a veil had been attached beneath, trailing the length of her dress behind her.

By the time Macie reached the front of the chapel, Holt's eyes were burning with emotion. He wanted the ceremony sped up so that he could take her in his arms and kiss her as his wife.

Ruby grabbed Macie's hand, so that she was standing between them, linking them together.

"Ruby, come here," Evie whispered.

Ruby adamantly shook her head.

"It's okay," Macie told Evie, then she met Holt's gaze.

He nodded. It was okay. Because he had vows to make to both of them.

The reverend began with his welcome and introduction, then he ran through the standard vows. Lane had told Holt to write his down, but every time he'd tried, there were just too many things he wanted to say. So he decided he would do it off the cuff, and that would likely be more from his heart anyway.

The reverend nodded for Holt to begin.

First, he knelt in front of Ruby and took her hand. "Hi, little darlin'," he said. "You look real pretty today."

Ruby smiled, her brown eyes crinkling.

"And since today's a very special day for me and your mother, I wanted to say a few things to you first."

"Okay, Holt."

He chuckled, then said, "You know you're my little darlin', and I also want you to know that I'm honored to be your stepdad. I hope that you'll always be able to ask me for

218

help, with anything, and know that I'll never turn you away. The most important thing in my life is taking care of you and your mother."

Ruby nodded.

"I love you, little darlin', and I hope you'll always feel that."

Ruby threw her arms about his neck, nearly shifting him off balance.

"I love you, too, Holt!"

He grinned and pulled her close, then when he finally released her, he rose and faced his almost-bride.

Macie wiped at the tears on her face with a shaking hand.

Holt released a breath. "Darling Macie," he began.

She gave him a trembling smile.

The sounds of the church and the eyes of the congregation faded until he only saw Macie. "You're the love of my life," he continued, "and I'm the luckiest man on earth today."

Her beautiful brown eyes gazed back at him, loving, and more importantly, trusting.

"I promise to always care for you, to cherish you," he said. "I promise to never forsake you and to spend the rest of my days serving you." He might have said other things, but it all turned into a blur.

When it was Macie's turn, she pulled out a paper tucked into her bouquet. "I needed a list," she said with a soft laugh.

Others around them smiled, and Macie wiped at her tears, then unfolded the paper. "To my love, Holt Prosper. When I was a little girl, I dreamed of marrying someday in a church full of summer flowers, while wearing a white dress and standing across from a handsome man. What I didn't know was that sometimes life takes unexpected detours." She sniffled, then continued, "Some of those days have been very hard and dark, but ever since I saw you at the airport on that summer day in June, my world has become brighter and brighter every day."

She met his gaze. "Thank you for being the light in my life, Holt, and thank you for loving me and my little girl. My love for you is without limit or depth, and I can only hope that I'll always live worthy of it." Tears dripped on her paper as she folded it.

When she looked up again, Holt said, "I love you, darlin'."

"I love you, too," she whispered.

The reverend jumped in and pronounced them man and wife, and it was a good thing, too, because Holt was tired of not kissing his sweetheart.

The words, "And you may now kiss your bride," were barely uttered when Holt closed the distance and slid his hand behind her neck. Then he lowered his head to hers and kissed her.

Applause erupted around them, but Holt continued kissing Macie. She clutched at his tuxedo lapels, and didn't seem to mind their audience.

Finally, he broke it off, if only to move along the rest of the wedding events. Keeping ahold of Macie's hand on one side, and Ruby's on his other side, they turned to the congregation. Another countdown had begun in his mind. They'd be arriving at an exclusive bed and breakfast retreat for their honeymoon in two hours and ten minutes. A place recommended by Kellie. And a place where Holt planned to prove to Macie how much she meant to him. He would show her how a true man treats his wife.

"Ready, darlin'?" he asked.

Macie squeezed his hand, her gaze flicking to his face. "I sure am."

He might have stolen another kiss or two before they began the walk up the aisle, out of the church, and into their new life. Together.

Heather B. Moore is a four-time *USA Today* bestselling author. She writes historical thrillers under the pen name H.B. Moore; her latest thrillers include *The Killing Curse* and *Breaking Jess*. Under the name Heather B. Moore, she writes romance and women's fiction. Her newest releases include the historical romances *Love is Come* and *Ruth*. She's also one of the coauthors of the *USA Today* bestselling series: A Timeless Romance Anthology. Heather writes speculative fiction under the pen name Jane Redd; releases include the Solstice series and *Mistress Grim*. Heather is represented by Dystel, Goderich & Bourret.

For book updates, sign up for Heather's email list:
hbmoore.com/contact
Website: HBMoore.com
Facebook: Fans of H. B. Moore
Blog: MyWritersLair.blogspot.com
Instagram: @authorhbmoore
Pinterest: HeatherBMoore
Twitter: @HeatherBMoore